Summer Bridge Activities®

Teacher Recommended!

BRIDGING GRADES

5 to 6

CARSON-DELLOSA™
PUBLISHING GROUP

Greensboro, NC 27425 USA

Caution: Exercise activities may require adult supervision. Before beginning any exercise activity, consult a physician. Written parental permission is suggested for those using this book in group situations. Children should always warm up prior to beginning any exercise activity and should stop immediately if they feel any discomfort during exercise.

Caution: Before beginning any food activity, ask parents' permission and inquire about the child's food allergies and religious or other food restrictions.

Caution: Nature activities may require adult supervision. Before beginning any nature activity, ask parents' permission and inquire about the child's plant and animal allergies. Remind the child not to touch plants or animals during the activity without adult supervision.

Caution: Before completing any balloon activity, ask parents' permission and inquire about possible latex allergies. Also, remember that uninflated or popped balloons may present a choking hazard.

The authors and publisher are not responsible or liable for any injury that may result from performing the exercises or activities in this book.

Summer Bridge™
An imprint of Carson-Dellosa Publishing LLC
PO Box 35665
Greensboro, NC 27425 USA
carsondellosa.com

Printed in the USA • All rights reserved.
05-016171151

ISBN 978-1-4838-1585-5

Table of Contents

About Summer Learning

Did you know that many students experience learning loss when they do not engage in educational activities during the summer? This means that some of what they have spent time learning over the preceding school year is forgotten during the summer months. However, summer learning loss is something that you can help prevent. Below are a few suggestions for fun and engaging activities that can help students maintain and grow their academic skills during the summer.

- Encourage your student to read for pleasure every day. Visit your local library together and select books on a variety of subjects that interest your child.

- Ask your child's teacher to recommend books for summer reading.

- Explore parks, nature preserves, museums, and cultural centers.

- Look for teachable moments every day. Measuring ingredients for recipes and reviewing maps before a car trip are fun and useful ways to learn or reinforce skills.

- Each day, set goals for your student to accomplish. For example, complete five math problems or read one section or chapter in a book.

- Encourage your student to complete the activities in this book regularly to help bridge the summer learning gap.

About Summer Bridge Activities®

The learning activities in this book are designed to review fifth grade skills, preview the skills your child will learn in sixth grade, and help prevent summer learning loss. Your involvement in your child's education is crucial to his or her success. Together with *Summer Bridge Activities*, you can fill the summer months with learning experiences that will deepen and enrich your child's knowledge and prepare him or her for the upcoming school year. Inside this book, you will find the following helpful resources:

Three sections that correspond to the three months of a traditional summer vacation. Each section begins with a goal-setting activity, a word list, and information about the fitness and character development activities located throughout the section.

Learning activity pages. For maximum results, your student should complete two activity pages each day. These engaging, age-appropriate activities cover a range of subjects including reading comprehension, writing, grammar skills, fractions, ratios, geometry, statistics, and more. Each page is numbered by day.

Bonus outdoor learning experiences, science experiments, and social studies exercises. These fun and creative activities are found at the end of each section. Encourage your child to complete the pages throughout each month as time allows.

Flash cards. Help your child cut out these handy cards and use them for practice anytime and anywhere. For students who are entering sixth grade, use the cards to:

- Learn words with Latin and Greek roots.
- Solve word analogies.
- Identify figures of speech such as metaphors and proverbs.
- Solve rate, ratio, and percent problems.
- Find greatest common factors and least common multiples.
- Compare positive and negative numbers.
- Evaluate algebraic expressions.
- Calculate area and volume.

Certificate of completion. At the end of the summer, fill out the certificate and present it to your child to celebrate learning success!

Online companion. Visit *summerlearningactivities.com/sba* with your child to find even more fun and creative ways to prevent summer learning loss.

Skills Matrix

Day	Addition & Subtraction	Algebra	Capitalization & Punctuation	Character Development	Critical Thinking	Data Analysis	Decimals, Fractions, & Percentages	Fitness	Geometry & Measurement	Grammar	Language Arts	Multiplication & Division	Numbers	Parts of Speech	Problem Solving	Reading Comprehension	Science	Sentence Structure & Types	Social Studies	Vocabulary & Spelling	Writing
1	★											★								★	
2										★			★	★					★		
3										★	★					★					
4									★											★	★
5							★	★						★						★	
6							★							★		★					
7					★							★								★	★
8														★	★		★			★	
9									★			★				★					
10				★								★		★							
11		★										★		★						★	
12									★					★						★	★
13		★							★					★		★					
14			★												★					★	★
15						★		★			★									★	
16							★							★	★						
17													★	★						★	
18												★	★				★			★	
19							★							★		★					
20			★				★					★								★	
						★				**BONUS PAGES!**							★		★	★	★
1		★					★									★				★	
2							★									★				★	
3							★						★						★	★	
4							★	★			★		★								
5							★			★						★					
6							★						★	★							★
7						★														★	★
8										★	★					★					
9			★							★				★						★	
10						★				★	★						★				
11	★									★	★					★					

© Carson-Dellosa

Skills Matrix

Day	Addition & Subtraction	Algebra	Capitalization & Punctuation	Character Development	Critical Thinking	Data Analysis	Decimals, Fractions, & Percentages	Fitness	Geometry & Measurement	Grammar	Language Arts	Multiplication & Division	Numbers	Parts of Speech	Problem Solving	Reading Comprehension	Science	Sentence Structure & Types	Social Studies	Vocabulary & Spelling	Writing
12		★									★	★									★
13		★								★	★	★									
14												★				★			★		
15			★								★			★			★				
16		★							★				★			★					
17												★		★		★					
18							★				★						★	★			
19						★					★	★									★
20		★														★				★	
						★	★		★	**BONUS PAGES!**							★		★		
1									★	★				★		★					
2										★				★	★						★
3							★									★				★	
4		★						★									★			★	
5		★				★														★	
6							★							★	★						
7									★		★										
8									★							★					
9			★						★							★					
10									★		★						★				★
11		★								★								★	★		
12							★									★				★	
13			★			★														★	
14						★								★			★	★			
15						★										★		★			
16			★						★		★						★			★	
17								★			★			★					★		
18						★							★			★					
19									★	★	★										★
20									★	★	★						★				
						★				**BONUS PAGES!**			★				★	★	★		★

Encouraging Summer Reading

Literacy is the single most important skill that your child needs to be successful in school. The following list includes ideas for ways that you can help your child discover the great adventures of reading!

- Establish a time for reading each day. Ask your child about what he or she is reading. Try to relate the material to a summer event or to another book.

- Let your child see you reading for enjoyment. Talk about the great things that you discover when you read.

- Create a summer reading list. Choose books from the reading list (pages ix–x) or head to the library and explore. Ask your child to read a page from a book aloud. If he or she does not know more than five words on the page, the book may be too difficult.

- Read newspaper and magazine articles, recipes, menus, and maps on a daily basis to show your child the importance of reading informational texts.

- Choose a nonfiction book from the reading list that gives a secondhand account of an event or of a person's life, such as the biography *Out of Darkness: The Story of Louis Braille*. Then, search at the library to find a firsthand account or eyewitness report of the same events. From what point of view are the two accounts told? How are the accounts similar? How are they different?

- Choose a nonfiction book to read or reread with your child. Then, have him or her pretend to be a TV reporter, sharing the "news" of the book you read. Encourage your child to relate details and events from the story in the report.

- Make up stories. This is especially fun to do in the car, on camping trips, or while waiting at the airport. Encourage your child to tell a story with a beginning, a middle, and an end. Or, have your child start a story and let other family members build on it.

- Encourage your child to join a summer reading club at the library or a local bookstore. Your child may enjoy talking to other children about the books that he or she has read.

- Encourage your child to read several books from a favorite genre, such as mystery or science fiction. Discuss how different books treat similar themes.

- Ask your child to think about a favorite character from a book or series of books. How might that character respond to different situations?

Summer Reading List

The summer reading list includes fiction and nonfiction titles. Experts recommend that fifth- and sixth-grade students read for at least 30 minutes each day. After your child reads, ask questions about the story to reinforce comprehension.

Decide on an amount of daily reading time for each month. You may want to write the time on the Monthly Goals page at the beginning of each section in this book.

Fiction

Avi
Windcatcher

Babbitt, Natalie
Tuck Everlasting

Barshaw, Ruth McNally
The Ellie McDoodle Diaries: New Kid in School

Blume, Judy
Freckle Juice

Brink, Carol Ryrie
Caddie Woodlawn

Burnett, Frances Hodgson
The Secret Garden

Cleary, Beverly
Dear Mr. Henshaw

Clements, Andrew
Frindle
Lunch Money

Colfer, Eoin
Artemis Fowl

Collins, Suzanne
Gregor the Overlander

Conrad, Pam
Pedro's Journal: A Voyage with Christopher Columbus August 3, 1492–February 14, 1493

Creech, Sharon
The Boy on the Porch

Dahl, Roald
Charlie and the Great Glass Elevator
Matilda

DiCamillo, Kate
The Tale of Despereaux

Fitzhugh, Louise
Harriet the Spy

Gardiner, John Reynolds
Stone Fox

George, Jean Craighead
My Side of the Mountain

Giff, Patricia Reilly
Winter Sky

Harper, Charise Mericle
Just Grace

Hill, Kirkpatrick
Bo at Ballard Creek

Horowitz, Anthony
Stormbreaker: The Graphic Novel adapted by Antony Johnston

Kinney, Jeff
Diary of a Wimpy Kid

MacLachlan, Patricia
Sarah, Plain and Tall

Summer Reading List (continued)

Fiction (continued)

Naylor, Phyllis Reynolds
Shiloh

Palacio, R. J.
Wonder

Paterson, Katherine
The Great Gilly Hopkins

Polacco, Patricia
Pink and Say

Rowling, J. K.
Harry Potter and the Sorcerer's Stone

Ryan, Pam Muñoz
Esperanza Rising

Sachar, Louis
Holes

Salisbury, Graham
Under the Blood-Red Sun

Selden, George
The Cricket in Times Square

Snicket, Lemony
The Bad Beginning, or Orphans!

Spinelli, Jerry
Maniac Magee

Standiford, Natalie
The Secret Tree

Wilder, Laura Ingalls
Little House on the Prairie

Williams-Garcia, Rita
P.S. Be Eleven

Nonfiction

Colbert, David
Thomas Edison (10 Days)

Curlee, Lynn
Trains

Fleischman, John
Phineas Gage: A Gruesome but True Story About Brain Science

Freedman, Russell
Out of Darkness: The Story of Louis Braille

Montgomery, Sy
Quest for the Tree Kangaroo: An Expedition to the Cloud Forest of New Guinea

Murphy, Jim
An American Plague: The True and Terrifying Story of the Yellow Fever Epidemic of 1793

Old, Wendie
To Fly: The Story of the Wright Brothers

Ryan, Pam Muñoz
When Marian Sang

Tan, Shaun
The Bird King

Turner, Pamela
The Dolphins of Shark Bay

Wick, Walter
A Drop of Water

Monthly Goals

A goal is something that you want to accomplish and must work toward. Sometimes, reaching a goal can be difficult.

Think of three goals to set for yourself this month. For example, you may want to exercise for 30 minutes each day. Write your goals on the lines. Post them someplace visible, where you will see them every day.

Draw a line through each goal as you meet it. Feel proud that you have met your goals and set new ones to continue to challenge yourself.

1. _____

2. _____

3. _____

Word List

The following words are used in this section. Use a dictionary to look up each word that you do not know. Then, write three sentences. Use a word from the word list in each sentence.

biome   physician
collide   porous
famished   sensible
fantasy   slogan
geyser   superb

1. _____

_____

2. _____

_____

3. _____

_____

I

Introduction to Flexibility

This section includes fitness and character development activities that focus on flexibility. These activities are designed to get you moving and thinking about building your physical fitness and your character.

Physical Flexibility

To the average person, *flexibility* means being able to accomplish everyday physical tasks easily, like bending to tie a shoe. These everyday tasks can be difficult for people whose muscles and joints have not been used and stretched regularly.

Proper stretching allows muscles and joints to move through their full range of motion, which is important for good flexibility. There are many ways that you stretch every day without realizing it. When you reach for a dropped pencil or a box of cereal on the top shelf, you are stretching your muscles. Flexibility is important to your health and growth, so challenge yourself to improve your flexibility. Simple stretches and activities, such as yoga and tai chi, can improve your flexibility. Set a stretching goal for the summer, such as practicing daily until you can touch your toes.

Flexibility of Character

While it is important to have a flexible body, it is also important to be mentally flexible. Being mentally flexible means being open-minded to change. It can be disappointing when things do not go your way, but this is a normal reaction. Think of a time when unforeseen circumstances ruined your plans. Maybe your mother had to work one weekend, and you could not go to a baseball game with friends because you needed to babysit a younger sibling. How did you deal with this situation?

A large part of being mentally flexible is realizing that there will be situations in life in which unexpected things happen. Often, it is how you react to the circumstances that affects the outcome. Arm yourself with tools to be flexible, such as having realistic expectations, brainstorming solutions to make a disappointing situation better, and looking for good things that may have resulted from the initial disappointment.

Mental flexibility can take many forms. For example, being fair, respecting the differences of other people, and being compassionate are ways that you can practice mental flexibility. In difficult situations, remind yourself to be flexible, and you will reap the benefits of this important character trait.

Solve each problem.

1. $793 \times 27 =$ _____

2. $483 \times 175 =$ _____

3. $7,136 \div 8 =$ _____

4. $763,947 - 244,398 =$ _____

5. $8\overline{)9,696} =$ _____

6. $45\overline{)2,974} =$ _____

7. $63,459 - 21,365 =$ _____

8. $\$678.14 + \$990.27 =$ _____

9. $569,040 \div 8 =$ _____

10. $573 + 4,935 + 7,340 =$ _____

Circle the definition of the underlined word as it is used in the sentence.

11. Alexi was <u>upset</u> about her score on the spelling test.

    A. spilled or overturned   B. distressed or anxious

12. Place a cool <u>compress</u> on your head if you have a headache.

    A. a cloth pad   B. push together

13. Do you use vanilla <u>extract</u> in your pancake batter?

    A. take out   B. concentrated form

14. The <u>proceeds</u> from the bake sale will go toward our class field trip to a living history farm.

    A. money from a sale   B. moves forward

DAY 1

Add a prefix to each base word to make a new word. Use *mis-*, *re-*, *un-*, *non-*, or *pre-*.

EXAMPLE:

view _____**preview, review**_____

15. name_____

16. read_____

17. heat_____

18. sure_____

19. treat_____

20. fit_____

21. turn_____

22. call_____

23. stop_____

24. place_____

Find the value of each expression.

25. $(4 + 8) \times 10 =$ _____

26. $45 \div (6 - 3) =$ _____

27. $46 - [(24 \div 6) + 19] =$ _____

28. $(18 \div 2) \times (56 \div 7) =$ _____

29. $(3 \times 14) \div 7 =$ _____

30. $[(14 + 12) \times 2] \div 13 =$ _____

31. $125 - (5 \times 12) =$ _____

32. $(15 \times 4) \times (8 - 3) =$ _____

33. $16 \times [2 + (18 \div 3)] =$ _____

34. $13 + (84 \div 2) - (55 \div 11) =$ _____

35. $[(104 + 26) \div 2] \times 8 =$ _____

36. $5,500 - [86 + (728 \div .25)] =$ _____

FACTOID: Although people in Las Vegas live in the Mojave Desert, they use more water per day than any other city in the world.

4

Write each expanded number in standard form.

1. $(2 \times 1{,}000{,}000) + (6 \times 100{,}000) + (8 \times 10{,}000) + (5 \times 1{,}000) + (3 \times 100) + (2 \times 10) +$
$(2 \times 1) =$ _____

2. $(4 \times 100) + (7 \times 10) + (8 \times 1) + (5 \times \frac{1}{10}) + (3 \times \frac{1}{100}) =$ _____

3. $(2 \times 10{,}000{,}000) + (3 \times 1{,}000{,}000) + (4 \times 100{,}000) + (9 \times 1{,}000) + (3 \times 10) + (6 \times 1) =$

_____

4. $(2 \times 1{,}000) + (1 \times 100) + (1 \times 10) + (1 \times 1) + (9 \times \frac{1}{100}) + (7 \times \frac{1}{1{,}000}) =$ _____

5. $(3 \times 100) + (4 \times 1) + (8 \times \frac{1}{10}) + (4 \times \frac{1}{1{,}000}) =$ _____

6. $(1 \times 10{,}000{,}000) + (6 \times 1{,}000{,}000) + (5 \times 10{,}000) + (3 \times 1{,}000) + (2 \times 100) + (4 \times 10)$
$+ (5 \times 1) + (9 \times \frac{1}{10}) + (9 \times \frac{1}{100}) =$ _____

Write each standard number in expanded form.

7. 37,126,489.2 _____

_____

8. 2,069.044 _____

_____

Circle the prepositions in each sentence.

9. Gracie and Helen had not seen each other for 50 years.

10. "Tell me about Grandpa," said Randy.

11. They carried the water packs on their backs.

12. I would go into the garden, but it is muddy.

13. Tommy passed the peas to his mother.

14. We should meet somewhere beyond the city limits.

15. The lights activate automatically after sunset.

16. Please put an umbrella in the trunk.

17. Add pepper to the soup.

18. Erika waded into the stream and looked at the minnows.

DAY 2

Circle the word that correctly completes each sentence.

19.   One day, Wendy and Wilma decided to go (camp, camping, camped).

20.   They (pack, packing, packed) everything they needed in their truck.

21.   Then, they went to (hunt, hunting, hunted) for a good place to camp.

22.   After looking for a long time, they (pick, picking, picked) a great campsite.

23.   (Park, Parking, Parked) the truck was tricky because the ground was slippery.

24.   Wendy went (splash, splashing, splashed) through a big puddle.

Use an atlas to find the major North American city that is closest to each latitude and longitude.

25.   61°N, 150°W _____

26.   34°N, 118°W _____

27.   39°N, 95°W _____

28.   30°N, 90°W _____

29.   42°N, 83°W _____

30.   45°N, 76°W _____

31.   35°N, 107°W _____

32.   41°N, 74°W _____

33.   40°N, 83°W _____

34.   51°N, 114°W _____

FITNESS FLASH: Practice a V-sit. Stretch five times.

* See page ii.

DAY 3

Correct the subject/verb agreement errors in the passage.

Every Monday, students in Mrs. Verdan's class works with partners to complete math challenges. Each pair select its own work space. Jeremy and Melvin goes to the math center. Gregory and Leo likes the sunny table by the window. Hector and Jeff chooses chairs near the board. Lily and Masandra takes the round table near the door. Manny and Zoe grabs the soft seats in the library corner. Macon and Travis sits near the science center. All of the pairs has 45 minutes to solve the day's puzzle. Most of them finishes on time. They shares their solutions with the whole group. A few students meets with Mrs. Verdan after school. She explain the solutions and answer questions. Mrs. Verdan's students always enjoys the weekly math challenges.

Complete each proverb with a word from the word bank. Then, explain what the proverb means.

leap	cake	turn	spice	basket

1. Variety is the _____ of life.

   _____

2. You cannot have your _____ and eat it too.

   _____

3. Don't put all your eggs in one _____.

   _____

4. Look before you _____.

   _____

5. One good _____ deserves another.

   _____

DAY 3

Read the passage. Then, answer the questions.

The Eagle Has Landed

American astronauts Neil Armstrong and Buzz Aldrin were the first people to walk on the moon. Their Lunar Module (LM) left *Apollo 11* at 1:45 P.M. on July 20, 1969. "The Eagle has wings," Armstrong stated. At 3:46 P.M., the LM emerged from behind the moon. It was at an altitude of about 20 miles (32.2 km) from the moon. The astronauts had to make the all-important, final decision of whether to remain in orbit or to descend to the lunar surface.

At approximately 4:07 P.M., Armstrong pressed the button marked "Proceed." But, the computer-controlled guidance system was about to take Aldrin and Armstrong into a football-field-sized crater filled with big boulders and rocks. With only precious seconds to spare, Armstrong took manual control of the spacecraft. He found a clear area amid the menacing rock field below. "Houston," Armstrong radioed. "Tranquility base here. The Eagle has landed."

Armstrong was the first human being to set foot on the moon. As his left foot touched the lunar surface to take the first step, he spoke the now famous words, "That's one small step for [a] man, one giant leap for mankind."

6. What was Armstrong referring to when he said, "The Eagle has landed"?

   _____

7. The word *lunar* is used several times in the passage. What is another word

   for *lunar*? _____

8. Why does the author call the decision to land on the moon an "all-important,

   final decision"? _____

9. What was the significance of this mission to humankind? _____

   _____

10. What does this passage tell you about the type of men Armstrong and Aldrin

    were when they made this journey? _____

    _____

FACTOID: The average temperature on Jupiter is -234°F (-148°C).

Identify each figure using letters from the box. All but one figure will be identified by more than one word.

A. regular polygon   B. triangle   C. rhombus   D. kite
  E. quadrilateral   F. parallelogram   G. hexagon   H. rectangle
                         I. square   J. trapezoid

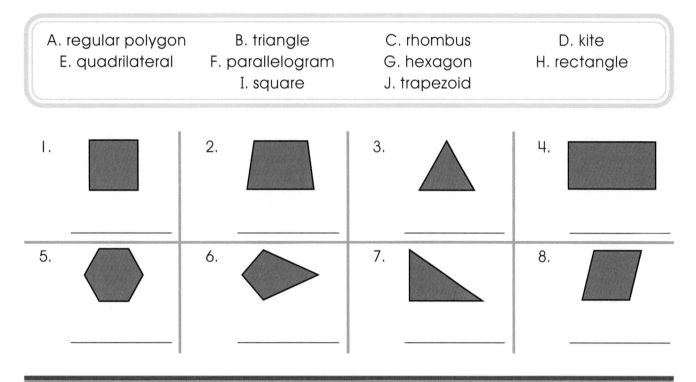

1. _____

2. _____

3. _____

4. _____

5. _____

6. _____

7. _____

8. _____

Circle a word to match each description. Underline its root.

9.   Which word contains a Greek root that means "earth"?

    spectacle   automobile   geography

10. Which word contains a Latin root that means "carry"?

    prediction   transportation   inspect

11. Which word contains a Latin root that means "drag or pull"?

    inject   tripod   extract

12. Which word contains a Greek root that means "the study of"?

    meteorology   structure   telegraph

13. Which word contains a Greek root that means "skin"?

    moped   dermatology   aggression

14. Which word contains a Latin root that means "ten"?

    trilogy   monologue   December

DAY 4

Add a prefix, suffix, or both to each base word. Write the meaning of the new word on the line.

15. _____ agree _____ _____

16. _____ placed _____

17. _____ respect _____ _____

18. _____ capable _____

19. avoid _____ _____

20. _____ change _____

21. delay _____ _____

22. _____ number _____ _____

23. loyal _____ _____

24. hazard _____ _____

25. care _____ _____

26. _____ depend _____ _____

A *limerick* is a humorous five-line poem with a set rhyme scheme, AABBA. This means that the first, second, and fifth lines rhyme and the third and fourth lines rhyme. Write a limerick about your summer vacation.

_____

_____

_____

_____

_____

_____

_____

FITNESS FLASH: Touch your toes 10 times.

* See page ii.

Read each number and answer the question.

1. **325,251.58**

   Which digit is in the thousands place? _____

2. **1,547.489**

   Which digit is in the thousandths place? _____

3. **348,019.57**

   Which digit is in the ten thousands place? _____

4. **10,825.643**

   Which digit is in the tenths place? _____

5. **241,389,613**

   Which digit is in the hundred millions place? _____

6. **12,541,698.489**

   Which digit is in the hundredths place? _____

Correlative conjunctions **join similar words, phrases, or clauses. Circle the correlative conjunctions in each sentence.**

7. Last night, both Dion and Noreen won awards.

8. Just as cars follow street signs, so must bikes.

9. Neither the map nor the itinerary fit in Ophelia's scrapbook.

10. We could use either molasses or sugar to sweeten the cookies.

11. Bea not only decorated the cupcakes but also made them from scratch.

12. Neither Carlos nor Mirabel is going to the meeting tonight.

13. Either a period or a semicolon can correct a run-on sentence.

14. Whether it rains or not, we will play soccer.

15. Both the paper and the project are due on Friday.

16. Mr. Oliver said that I can either bring my own pencil or borrow one.

DAY 5

Study the list of prefixes and suffixes and their meanings. Then, write the meaning of each word.

Prefixes		Suffixes	
re-	back or again	**-ment**	the act, result, or product of
dis-	away, apart, or the opposite of	**-ish**	of or belonging to; like or about
un-	opposite, not, or lack of	**-less**	without or not
pre-	before		

17. punishment _____

18. disappear _____

19. presoak _____

20. rewind _____

21. colorless _____

22. precooked _____

23. unsure _____

24. brownish _____

Balloon Ballet

How graceful are you? Ballet dancers are known to be very strong yet graceful. Their movements are flowing, and they are very flexible. Practicing a graceful walk across the floor like a ballet dancer helps stress good posture. Inflate a balloon and place it on your head. Without looking down, walk on the balls of your feet with your arms above your head. If you can make it several steps without dropping the balloon, you are practicing graceful control.

> **CHARACTER CHECK:** Think of a game you like to play. Write a song, story, or poem promoting fairness in playing the game.

* See page ii.

Solve. Write answers in simplest form.

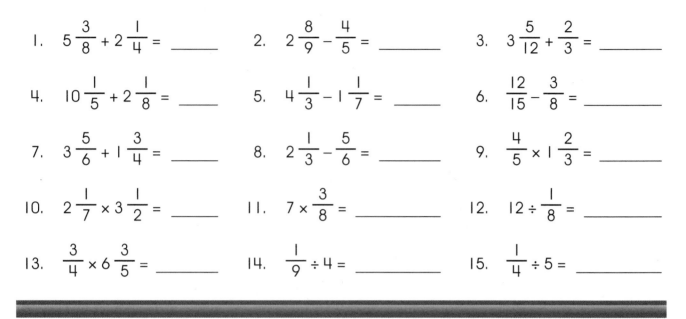

1. $5\dfrac{3}{8} + 2\dfrac{1}{4} =$ _____

2. $2\dfrac{8}{9} - \dfrac{4}{5} =$ _____

3. $3\dfrac{5}{12} + \dfrac{2}{3} =$ _____

4. $10\dfrac{1}{5} + 2\dfrac{1}{8} =$ _____

5. $4\dfrac{1}{3} - 1\dfrac{1}{7} =$ _____

6. $\dfrac{12}{15} - \dfrac{3}{8} =$ _____

7. $3\dfrac{5}{6} + 1\dfrac{3}{4} =$ _____

8. $2\dfrac{1}{3} - \dfrac{5}{6} =$ _____

9. $\dfrac{4}{5} \times 1\dfrac{2}{3} =$ _____

10. $2\dfrac{1}{7} \times 3\dfrac{1}{2} =$ _____

11. $7 \times \dfrac{3}{8} =$ _____

12. $12 \div \dfrac{1}{8} =$ _____

13. $\dfrac{3}{4} \times 6\dfrac{3}{5} =$ _____

14. $\dfrac{1}{9} \div 4 =$ _____

15. $\dfrac{1}{4} \div 5 =$ _____

Combine each pair of sentences using a coordinating conjunction from the word bank. In compound sentences, use a comma before the coordinating conjunction.

and	but	for	or	so	yet

16. Devin went swimming in the pool. He did not go swimming in the lake.

_____

_____

17. She enjoys making art. She chooses to spend more time playing sports.

_____

_____

18. Josie picked up her backpack. She got on the bus.

_____

_____

19. We can watch the movie. We can meet Joe at the park.

_____

_____

DAY 6

Read the passage. Then, answer the questions.

Biomes of Canada

Canada has many different **biomes**, or ecosystems. Some of the southern provinces are covered in grasslands. The Hudson Plains, near Hudson Bay, contain one-quarter of Earth's wetlands, which attract many migrating birds. Much of southern Canada is covered by the Boreal Shield, which includes forests and rivers that were once used for fur trade. Far northern Canada is covered by tundra, which contains permanently frozen ground called *permafrost*. Much of western Canada is within a mountain biome. The far southeastern provinces are in the Atlantic Maritime biome. *Maritime* refers to the sea. This area receives heavy rainfall because it is near the Atlantic Ocean. Along Canada's border with the U.S. state of Alaska lie temperate rain forests. Because this area is near the Pacific Ocean, its climate is very mild. The smallest biome, a temperate deciduous forest, contains half of Canada's population and the cities of Toronto and Montreal.

20. What is the main idea of this passage?
    A. Some biomes are mountainous, and others have grasslands.
    B. Many people live in Toronto and Montreal.
    C. Canada has a variety of climates and landscapes.

21. What is a biome? _____

22. Name three biomes that can be found in Canada. _____
    _____

23. What is permanently frozen ground called? _____

24. Why does the Atlantic Maritime biome have heavy rainfall? _____
    _____

25. Which area in Canada contains one-quarter of Earth's wetlands?
    _____

26. What does the term *maritime* refer to? _____

27. What kinds of biomes are found in the United States? Do some research to determine how they are similar to and different from the biomes of Canada. Write a paragraph about your findings on a separate sheet of paper.

Find each quotient. Round answers to the nearest thousandth.

1. 8)231

2. 5)3,305

3. 75)9,283

4. 4)394

5. 75)675

6. 40)7,384

7. 9)894

8. 70)5,824

Write a review of a book you have read, telling whether you liked it or disliked it. State your opinion clearly and give specific reasons to support it. Then, visit an online bookstore with an adult. Look up the book you reviewed and read reviews that others have written. How does your opinion of the book compare to others' opinions?

_____

_____

_____

_____

_____

_____

_____

_____

_____

_____

_____

_____

DAY 7

Write the letter of each definition next to the correct word.

9.	_____ geyser	A.	not in favor of
10.	_____ advice	B.	writing instrument
11.	_____ generate	C.	produce
12.	_____ slogan	D.	control
13.	_____ pencil	E.	operation
14.	_____ regulate	F.	make hard contact
15.	_____ collide	G.	hot spring
16.	_____ gelatin	H.	motto
17.	_____ surgery	I.	recommendation
18.	_____ against	J.	jellylike substance

There are four trees in the park. The ages of the trees are 18 years, 27 years, 45 years, and 48 years. Use the clues and the table below to find the age of each tree.

- The maple tree is planted beside the oldest tree.
- The pine tree is not the youngest tree.
- The oldest tree has the shortest name.
- The youngest tree is planted across from the maple tree.
- The second youngest tree never has leaves.

		18 years	27 years	45 years	48 years
19.	Maple				
20.	Pine				
21.	Birch				
22.	Oak				

FITNESS FLASH: Do arm circles for 30 seconds.

* See page ii.

Solve each problem. Write answers in simplest form.

1. Connor picked $8\frac{1}{5}$ pounds of apples. Louisa picked $9\frac{2}{3}$ pounds of apples. How many more pounds of apples did Louisa pick than Connor?

_____ pounds

2. Tabitha is $4\frac{7}{12}$ feet tall. Her father is $1\frac{4}{7}$ feet taller. How tall is Tabitha's father?

_____ feet tall

3. Ben watched a play. The first act was $\frac{5}{6}$ hours long. The intermission was $\frac{1}{4}$ hour long. The second act was $1\frac{1}{5}$ hours long. How long was Ben at the play altogether?

_____ hours

4. Marcus watched a soccer match for $2\frac{1}{5}$ hours. Drew watched a football game for $3\frac{3}{8}$ hours. How much longer was the football game than the soccer match?

_____ hours

Circle the action verbs. Underline the linking verbs.

walk	seem	is	cry	became
sound	wore	sneezed	become	blew
call	being	read	built	clapped
dance	will	eat	have been	watched
are	gather	cheer	was	wants
be	were	am	speak	have
sit	throw	meowing	has	mopped
caught	jump	barking	carried	had
been	won	selling	has had	hit
honked	dive	climbs	bake	helped
smell	rolled	skiing	wash	carried
plays	wiggled	paint	practice	fed

DAY 8

Write a word from the word bank to complete each sentence.

allergies	conduct	inlets	frank	stethoscope
suspicious	knead	subscribe	margin	owes

5. The doctor listened to my heart through the _____.

6. The night watchman became _____ of the parked car.

7. We _____ to at least four newspapers.

8. Did you leave a _____ on each side of your paper?

9. Ted always _____ someone money.

10. She was _____ in telling me that the movie was too long.

11. Use both hands when you _____ the bread dough.

12. Three of my classmates have food _____.

13. Toby's _____ at the recital was extremely good.

14. All of the _____ around the lake were crowded with boats.

Matter exists in three states: solid, liquid, and gas. Write each word from the word bank under the correct heading.

air	box	dust	helium	hydrogen	ice
juice	lava	milk	oxygen	rock	water

Solid	**Liquid**	**Gas**
_____	_____	_____
_____	_____	_____
_____	_____	_____
_____	_____	_____

FACTOID: Gideon Sundback invented the zipper in 1913.

Use mental math to find each product.

1. 0.07 × 10 = _____
2. 16 × 10 = _____
3. 10 × 9.2 = _____
4. 100 × 80 = _____
5. 50 × 0.50 = _____
6. 7 × 600 = _____
7. 500 × 0.20 = _____
8. 5 × 900 = _____
9. 70 × 0.06 = _____
10. 30 × 400 = _____
11. 200 × 0.3 = _____
12. 400 × 600 = _____
13. 8 × 1,000 = _____
14. 0.9 × 3,000 = _____
15. 30 × 5,000 = _____

Circle the form of the verb *to be* that correctly completes each sentence.

16. I (be, am) guessing the number of pennies in the jar.

17. What (is, be) your favorite month?

18. The workmen (been, were) repairing the road in front of our house.

19. Carla (was, were) laughing very loudly.

20. (Is, Are) you the team leader?

21. My Uncle Caleb (been, has been, have been) an astronaut for many years.

22. The old house (is being, are being) torn down.

23. We (be, will be) playing in the orchestra on Saturday night.

Write a sentence using each form of the verb *to be*. Make sure that your sentences are different from the ones above.

24. were _____

25. has been _____

26. was being _____

27. are _____

FACTOID: There are more than 1.2 billion teenagers in the world.

DAY 9

Read the passage. Then, answer the questions.

The Lost Colony

Englishman Sir Walter Raleigh wanted to start a colony in the New World (North America). In 1585, Raleigh sent colonists to what is now North Carolina. The colonists did not want to work and almost starved to death. They were taken back to England. Two years later, a second group of colonists sailed to the same place as the previous colonists. They worked very hard to survive.

Because of a war involving England, Raleigh lost track of the colonists. In 1591, a ship from England arrived to check on the colonists, but the colonists had disappeared! There was no sign of life. All that the sailors found were some empty trunks, rotted maps, and the word CROATAN carved on the door post of the fort. Croatan was an island 100 miles south of the Lost Colony. No one knows whether the colonists were attacked by the Croatan Indians or whether the colonists went to live on Croatan Island. The Lost Colony has been a great mystery in American history.

28. Where is the Lost Colony? _____

29. How many years did it take Sir Walter Raleigh to send a ship to check on the second group of colonists? _____

30. Why do you think this colony was called the *Lost Colony*? _____

_____

31. Find another account of the Lost Colony online. How is it different from the passage above? Is it told from a different point of view? Write a letter or an e-mail to a relative telling what you learned from both sources about the Lost Colony.

FITNESS FLASH: Do 10 shoulder shrugs.

* See page ii.

Find each product.

1.   826
   × 47

2.   584
   × 29

3.   249
   × 63

4.   973
   × 51

5.   628
   × 274

6.   831
   × 347

7.   609
   × 149

8.   586
   × 781

Write the past-tense form of each irregular verb in parentheses to complete each sentence.

EXAMPLE:

I (wear) _____**wore**_____ an old coat to school.

9.   The telephone (ring) _____ 10 times before she answered it.

10. The contractor (build) _____ a new apartment building every year.

11. Aunt Dawn (feed) _____ her cats three times a day.

12. We each (choose) _____ a friend to go with us to Funland.

13. My brother (spend) _____ all of his allowance on ice cream.

14. The top (spin) _____ for five minutes.

15. Our family (run)_____ in a marathon two summers ago.

16. I (awake) _____ when my dog jumped on my bed.

17. They (become) _____ excited when their team scored a point.

18. My uncle (bring) _____me a T-shirt from his trip.

19. My friend (draw) _____ a picture of me.

20. The starfish (grow) _____ a new arm.

DAY 10

An *interjection* is a word or phrase that shows surprise or another emotion. Underline each interjection and the punctuation following it.

21. OK, I understand this now.

22. Shh! We're trying to get our work done.

23. Ouch, get off my foot!

24. Wow! I passed!

25. Mmmm, something smells delicious!

26. Really, would you do that for me?

27. Stop! That isn't very nice.

28. Hold on, I'm almost finished.

29. Oops! I broke the lead on another pencil.

30. Hey, give that back!

Accepting Differences

Accepting differences means accepting another person's qualities and personality just as they are. At times, accepting differences might be challenging. It can become easier with practice, especially as you become more self-aware. Read the following situations. On a separate sheet of paper, write the possible outcomes of not accepting differences. Then, write the benefits of accepting differences.

- You have been assigned to work on a class project with a classmate. He and his family recently immigrated to the United States, and you do not know him well. All of your friends are in another group. The teacher has informed you that there will be no changes made to the groups. You must work with this person and create a project to present to the class by the end of the week.

- You are at a friend's house after school. The family insists that you stay for dinner. You agree. You sit down at the table and look at the food being served. You realize that the food looks and smells very different from your typical dinner at home.

CHARACTER CHECK: Write a 30-second commercial promoting honesty. Share it with a family member.

Estimate the amount of time it will take you to complete the 36 multiplication problems. Find each product. Time yourself.

Estimated Time:_____ Actual Time:_____ Difference Between the Two Times:_____

1. $6 \times 7 =$ _____
2. $8 \times 9 =$ _____
3. $5 \times 5 =$ _____
4. $11 \times 5 =$ _____
5. $12 \times 2 =$ _____
6. $6 \times 9 =$ _____
7. $9 \times 0 =$ _____
8. $9 \times 6 =$ _____
9. $5 \times 10 =$ _____
10. $11 \times 10 =$ _____
11. $9 \times 3 =$ _____
12. $9 \times 12 =$ _____
13. $12 \times 3 =$ _____
14. $10 \times 9 =$ _____
15. $7 \times 4 =$ _____
16. $6 \times 8 =$ _____
17. $7 \times 8 =$ _____
18. $9 \times 11 =$ _____
19. $12 \times 4 =$ _____
20. $7 \times 10 =$ _____
21. $11 \times 12 =$ _____
22. $7 \times 3 =$ _____
23. $9 \times 9 =$ _____
24. $5 \times 11 =$ _____
25. $7 \times 5 =$ _____
26. $12 \times 10 =$ _____
27. $7 \times 9 =$ _____
28. $10 \times 10 =$ _____
29. $11 \times 2 =$ _____
30. $12 \times 6 =$ _____
31. $8 \times 5 =$ _____
32. $6 \times 11 =$ _____
33. $10 \times 3 =$ _____
34. $8 \times 8 =$ _____
35. $10 \times 4 =$ _____
36. $12 \times 11 =$ _____

Write the past-tense form of each irregular verb in parentheses to complete each sentence.

37. The monkey (eat) _____ four bananas.

38. I was so afraid of the dark that I (shake) _____ when the lights went out.

39. Kai (hold) _____ his breath for one minute.

40. My nose (bleed) _____ for five minutes last night.

41. The students (write) _____ essays telling what they did on their field trip.

42. Alexander (ride) _____ his Shetland pony in the parade last summer.

43. Julie's mother (teach) _____ us how to jump double Dutch.

44. My sisters and I (fight) _____ a lot when we were children.

45. The rain (freeze) _____ when it hit the pavement.

DAY 11

Write the expression for each phrase.

46. 16 more than the quotient of 84 and 12

   _____

47. 14 less than the product of 12 and 7

   _____

48. the quotient of 63 and 9 multiplied by 7

   _____

49. the difference of 54 and 32 multiplied by the difference of 8 and 5

   _____

50. $\frac{1}{3}$ of 36 multiplied by the difference of 15 and 2

   _____

51. the difference of 28 and 4 divided by 6

   _____

Choose the word or phrase from the word bank that has almost the same meaning as the underlined word or phrase in each sentence.

cash crops	indigo
indentured servants	proprietor

_____ 52. George Calvert was the first <u>owner</u> of a colony.

_____ 53. Many Southern farmers grew <u>crops to sell for money</u>.

_____ 54. In 1744, Eliza Lucas developed <u>a blue dye made from a plant</u>.

_____ 55. Originally, <u>people who agreed to work five or seven years to pay their passage to America</u> labored on Southern farms.

FACTOID: Because the moon is 400 times closer to Earth than the sun, the moon and the sun appear to be the same size.

Find the volume of each cube.

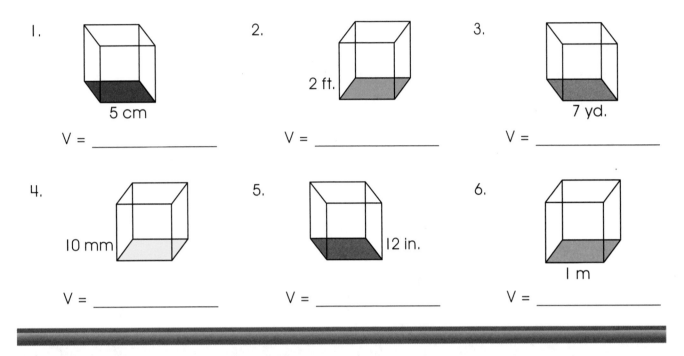

1.

5 cm

V = _____

2.

2 ft.

V = _____

3.

7 yd.

V = _____

4.

10 mm

V = _____

5.

12 in.

V = _____

6.

1 m

V = _____

To show the past tense of an irregular verb, change the spelling. In a sentence, the past participle is used with a helping verb. Write each irregular verb under the correct heading.

EXAMPLE: tear   tore   (have, has) torn

seen	rang	swum	eat	go	sung	swam
began	sing	rung	begin	went	begun	sang
swim	eaten	gone	ate	ring	see	saw

7.   Present

8.   Past

9.   Past Participle

_____ | _____ | _____

_____ | _____ | _____

_____ | _____ | _____

_____ | _____ | _____

_____ | _____ | _____

DAY 12

Circle the word that is misspelled in each row and spell it correctly on the line. Use a dictionary if you need help.

10.	refund	remodle	decode	preview	_____
11.	deposet	pretend	deflate	pace	_____
12.	mold	respond	giggel	revise	_____
13.	fiction	shelfes	unsafe	equip	_____
14.	transfer	defend	truthful	penlty	_____
15.	prdict	decide	gossip	fragile	_____
16.	beware	precice	porches	capital	_____
17.	leashes	cipher	estamate	climax	_____
18.	month	friendly	wrench	businiss	_____
19.	jiant	rectangle	guest	greet	_____

Invent a new ice-cream flavor. How is it made? What will you call it? Describe your new flavor.

_____

_____

_____

_____

_____

_____

_____

_____

_____

_____

FITNESS FLASH: Practice a V-sit. Stretch five times.

* See page ii.

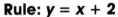

Use the rule to write the missing numbers. Then, write each coordinate pair (x, y) and plot the points on the coordinate plane. Draw a line through all the points.

Rule: $y = x + 2$

Point	x	y	(x, y)
A	1	3	(1, 3)
B	2	___	(___ , ___)
C	3	___	(___ , ___)
D	4	___	(___ , ___)
E	5	___	(___ , ___)
F	6	___	(___ , ___)
G	7	___	(___ , ___)

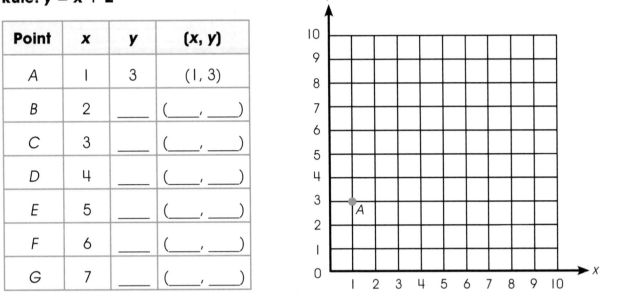

Write the future-tense form of each verb in parentheses to complete each sentence.

1. A group (build) _____ a huge rocket.

2. Technicians (check) _____ safety issues.

3. Ian and his dad (map) _____ the journey ahead of time.

4. Ian and his friends (board) _____ the rocket.

5. The announcer (count) _____ down to zero.

6. The rocket (launch) _____ into orbit.

7. The crew (view) _____ Earth from space.

8. They (observe) _____ comets and asteroids.

9. Marshall (record) _____ space sounds.

10. Emily (photograph) _____ interesting things.

Earth's History

Dinosaurs lived long ago—approximately 60 million years ago. Today, all that is left of them are their fossils, bones, and footprints. But, what does 60 million years mean to us? Scientists developed a geologic time scale that illustrates the periods in Earth's history. It can help those of us living today gain some perspective about the time involved in the development of life on Earth.

Read the chart. Then, answer the questions.

11. Earth's history is divided into how many major eras? _____

12. What are the names of the eras?

    _____

    _____

    _____

    _____

13. In which era did dinosaurs exist?

    _____

14. Into how many periods is the Mesozoic era divided? _____

15. What are the Mesozoic periods' names?

    _____

    _____

    _____

16. In which era do you live?

    _____

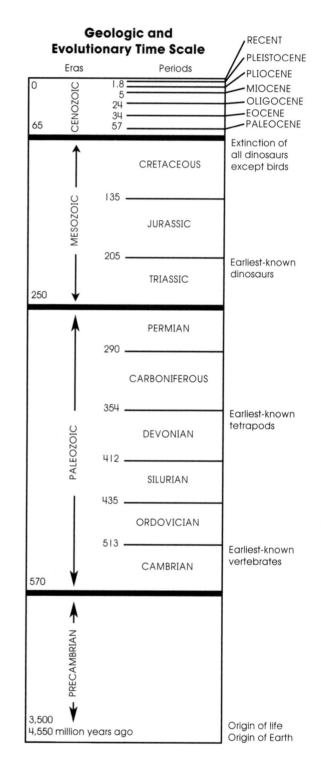

Geologic and Evolutionary Time Scale

FACTOID: Lithium is the lightest metal on Earth.

Eggs are classified primarily by their weight. A dozen small eggs weighs approximately 18 ounces. Medium eggs weigh 21 ounces a dozen. Large eggs weigh 24 ounces a dozen. Extra large eggs weigh a hefty 27 ounces a dozen. Jumbo eggs, which are classified as the largest salable eggs, weigh 30 ounces a dozen.

Use the information above to answer each question.

1. Six dozen _____ eggs weigh a total of 180 ounces.

2. Which weigh more, 3 dozen jumbo eggs or 6 dozen small eggs? _____

    _____

3. If 5 dozen eggs weigh 120 ounces total, which size are they? _____

4. What is the minimum weight you can have if you have 4 dozen eggs?

    _____ ounces of _____ eggs

5. If you bought a dozen of each size of egg, what would be the total weight

    in ounces? _____

Punctuate the title in each sentence correctly. Underline titles that would be italicized in type.

6. This summer, I read a great book, Stargirl by Jerry Spinelli.

7. Grandma Sheryl's favorite movie is The Wizard of Oz.

8. Amina borrowed Walk Two Moons and Wonder from the library.

9. The first song Chloe memorized for her role in the play Grease was Summer Nights.

10. What time does the next performance of Peter Pan begin?

11. The poem The Red Wheelbarrow was written by William Carlos Williams, who was a physician as well as a poet.

12. Jessy sang The Wheels on the Bus to the little boys she was baby-sitting.

13. I'll never forget the first time I saw Star Wars.

14. Our whole family enjoys watching the show Modern Family together.

DAY 14

Correct the journal entry. Cross out each misspelled word and rewrite the word correctly above it.

Febuary 8, 2015

Dear Journel,

It has definately been a busy weekend. My calender was completely full. On Friday morning, I opened the door after the doorbell rang. I was expecting to see my friend and naybor, Adrienne. Instead, I saw Aunt Carol. I was happy and suprised. There was not much time to talk. I had to leave for school in a few minutes, and Mom would head to the library in about an hour. "I took an early train," Aunt Carol explained. "I know everyone will be gone all day. Don't worry about me. I will clean out the cuboards and vacume the living room while your gone. We will catch up tonight. I especialy look forward to the priviledge of talking to you." Then, she gave me a big hug. We talked untill it was time to leave for school.

Write five questions that you would like to ask the leader of your country.

_____

_____

_____

_____

_____

_____

_____

_____

_____

FITNESS FLASH: Touch your toes 10 times.

* See page ii.

For a lab, Louis's science class is using 10 test tubes filled with different solutions. Louis used a line plot to show the liquid volume of each test tube. Use the data to answer the questions.

```
                        X
              X         X                   X        X        X
              X         X         X         X        X        X
    ←—————————————————————————————————————————————————————————————————————→
      60      61        62        63        64        65       66       67        68       69       70 ml
```

1. What is the total liquid volume of test tubes that contain less than 65 ml?

    _____

2. What is the total liquid volume of all 10 test tubes?

    _____

3. If the solutions from all 10 tubes were poured together and then redistributed evenly, how much liquid volume of solution would be in each test tube?

    _____

4. Louis wants to add water to the solutions so that each test tube contains 70 ml. How much water will he need for all 10?

    _____

The glossary below is from a kids' cookbook. Use it to answer the questions.

baste: to brush a liquid, such as fat or drippings, over meat during roasting
blanch: to immerse a fruit or vegetable in boiling water, remove it, and place it in a bowl of ice water
caramelize: to brown sugar over medium heat
dilute: to thin a liquid by adding more liquid, particularly milk or water
julienne: to cut food into long, thin strips

5. Give an example of a food you might blanch. _____

6. If you added an entry for the word *dredge*, where would you place it?

    _____

7. Alysha cut carrots and cucumbers into long strips. What is another word for this?

    _____

8. Would you be more likely to baste a strawberry cake or a pot roast?

    _____

DAY 15

Write a synonym for the word in parentheses to complete each sentence. Use a thesaurus if you need help.

EXAMPLE: I had to (finish) ____**complete**____ my work before I could go with my friends.

9.   Sarah and Angie go for a (walk) _____ every day except Sunday.

10.   It's fun to watch the little colts (play) _____ in the pasture.

11.   The electricians have done (enough) _____ work for this week.

12.   I cannot (find) _____ the information I need for my report.

13.   You should write all of the important events of your (trip) _____ .

14.   The lost couple had not had any (food) _____ for two days.

15.   Will you please (show) _____ how your new invention works?

16.   They will (try) _____ to climb Mount Everest again next summer.

17.   The Hubble Space Telescope (completes) _____ one orbit around Earth every 96 minutes.

18.   The value of this coin will (grow) _____ over the years.

Animal Stretch

Have you ever watched cats, dogs, or other animals stretch? Yoga is a practice of stretches that improve your body's flexibility and strength. Many common yoga poses are based on the movements of animals, such as dogs, cats, monkeys, and birds. Research your favorite animal. Then, create a stretch that mirrors the way your animal moves. If you need ideas, you may want to research some common yoga poses. Your stretch can be a seated stretch or a standing stretch. Share your move with a friend and see if she can perform your stretch. Can she guess what animal she is copying?

> **CHARACTER CHECK:** Look up the word *responsible* in the dictionary. How are you responsible?

* See page ii.

Circle the verb in parentheses that agrees with the subject of each sentence.

1. People (use, uses) various kinds of watercraft for fun.

2. Old-fashioned muscle power (propel, propels) some types of watercraft.

3. Some rafts (is, are) made by tying pieces of wood together.

4. Pacific Islanders (digs, dig) out tree trunks to make dugout canoes.

5. The world's largest dugout canoe (carry, carries) 70 people.

6. Boys and girls often (enjoy, enjoys) canoeing at summer camps.

7. One paddler (steer, steers) a type of canoe called a *kayak*.

8. The paddle (is, are) double-bladed.

More than one adjective can be used to modify the same noun. Underline the adjectives in each sentence. Then, circle the words they modify.

9. The wild, eerie wind frightened the children.

10. A fuzzy, brown caterpillar was creeping down the sidewalk.

11. Staci splashed some fresh, cool water on her face.

12. The hot, tired explorers swam in a large, clear lake.

13. The spicy aroma of apple cider filled Jason's small, warm tent.

An adjective that has the suffix _–er_ (comparative form) or _–est_ (superlative form) is used to compare nouns. Rewrite the adjective in parentheses by adding _–er_ or _–est_ to complete each sentence.

14. What is the (long) _____ word in the English dictionary?

15. Our back door is (wide) _____ than our front door.

16. Mozart was one of the world's (young) _____ composers.

17. The gorilla is the (large) _____ of all of the apes.

18. New Jersey is a (small) _____ state than Pennsylvania.

DAY 16

Read the passage. Then, answer the questions.

from *The Wind in the Willows* by Kenneth Grahame

The Mole had been working very hard all the morning, spring-cleaning his little home. First with brooms, then with dusters; then on ladders and steps and chairs, with a brush and a pail of whitewash; till he had dust in his throat and eyes, and splashes of whitewash all over his black fur, and an aching back and weary arms. Spring was moving in the air above and in the earth below and around him, **penetrating** even his dark and lowly little house with its spirit of divine discontent and longing. It was small wonder, then, that he suddenly flung down his brush on the floor, said 'Bother!' and 'O blow!' and also 'Hang spring-cleaning!' and bolted out of the house without even waiting to put on his coat. Something up above was calling him imperiously, and he made for the steep little tunnel which answered in his case to the gravelled carriage-drive owned by animals whose residences are nearer to the sun and air. So he scraped and scratched and scrabbled and scrooged and then he scrooged again and scrabbled and scratched and scraped, working busily with his little paws and muttering to himself, 'Up we go! Up we go!' till at last, pop! his snout came out into the sunlight, and he found himself rolling in the warm grass of a great meadow.

19. What does the word *penetrating* mean in the story?

    _____

20. Find an example of alliteration in the passage and write it on the lines. How does it contribute to the story? _____

    _____

    _____

21. How does Grahame create the character of the mole? What details help paint a picture of his personality? _____

    _____

    _____

FACTOID: A camel can drink up to 25 gallons of water in 10 minutes.

Solve each problem. Write answers in simplest form.

1. Nola studied for her math test three times yesterday. She studied for $\frac{1}{4}$ hour in the morning, $1\frac{3}{8}$ hours after school, and $\frac{1}{2}$ hour before bed. How long did she study altogether?

_____ hours

2. The grocer put $3\frac{1}{3}$ pounds of potatoes on the scale. Then, he removed a potato weighing $\frac{4}{5}$ pound. How much weight is on the scale now?

_____ pounds

3. A recipe calls for 2 cups of flour, $\frac{1}{4}$ cup of sugar, and $\frac{1}{3}$ cup of milk. What is the total volume of the three ingredients?

_____ cups

4. The distance between two towns is $12\frac{5}{8}$ miles. Mr. Lang has driven $4\frac{5}{12}$ miles of the distance. How much farther does he have left to go?

_____ miles

Write *PA* if the underlined word or group of words is a proper adjective. Write *PN* if the word or group of words is a proper noun.

5. _____ There are many <u>Puerto Rican</u> neighborhoods in New York City.

6. _____ Some people have recently arrived from <u>Puerto Rico</u>.

7. _____ Years ago, many <u>Italian</u> immigrants landed in America.

8. _____ People came from <u>Ireland</u> in the 1800s and 1900s.

9. _____ Some <u>German</u> people immigrated to America, too.

10. _____ Some of the first <u>English</u> settlers were the Puritans.

11. _____ They left <u>England</u> for several reasons in the 1600s.

12. _____ <u>Japanese</u> immigrants brought agricultural products such as tea plants and bamboo roots to the United States.

13. _____ <u>Chinese</u> immigration in the 1850s was fueled by the construction of

_____ the Transcontinental Railroad and the <u>California</u> gold rush.

DAY 17

Choose a word from the word bank that is a synonym for each bold word. Then, write it in the crossword puzzle.

Word Bank:
remember
well-known
starving
smart
great
crowd
doctor
grabbed
chew

Across

2. My **intelligent** dog learned a new trick.
3. Your party was **superb**!
4. Jack's puppy likes to **gnaw** on toys.
5. Do you **recall** the phone number?
6. I went to my **physician** when I got sick.

Down

1. On Monday, a **famous** artist will visit us.
2. I was **famished**, so I ate a snack.
3. My aunt **grasped** the railing as she came down the stairs.
4. A **mob** of fans was at the concert.

Below are some sentences about the first president of the United States, George Washington. Read the sentences and put them in the correct chronological order.

_____ When his father died in 1743, Washington went to live on a plantation known as Mount Vernon.

_____ George Washington was born in 1732 in Virginia.

_____ Washington married Martha Dandridge Custis in 1759.

_____ Washington became the first president of the United States in 1789.

_____ George Washington died in 1799.

_____ In 1758, Washington served in the Virginia House of Burgesses.

_____ Washington served in the French and Indian War from 1754–1758.

FITNESS FLASH: Do arm circles for 30 seconds.

* See page ii.

Solve each problem. Write answers in simplest form.

1. A single serving of pasta salad requires $\frac{1}{4}$ cup of dry pasta. How much pasta is needed for $9\frac{1}{2}$ servings?

_____ cups of dry pasta

2. Deepak stacked 14 copies of the same book. Each book is $1\frac{3}{8}$ inches thick. How high is the stack of books?

_____ inches

3. Megan has 5 yards of cloth to make napkins. She needs $\frac{1}{8}$ yard for each napkin. How many napkins can Megan make with the cloth?

_____ napkins

4. Trinity has 12 ounces of tea leaves. If each cup of tea requires $\frac{2}{3}$ ounce of tea leaves, how many cups of tea can Trinity make?

_____ cups of tea

Adverbs are words that modify or describe verbs, adjectives, and other adverbs. Adverbs tell *how, when*, and *where*. Many adverbs end with *-ly*. Write each adverb next to the question it answers.

above	carefully	eagerly	far	hard	here
immediately	inside	lately	quickly	never	often
softly	soon	there	today	upstairs	wildly

5. When?						
6. How?						
7. Where?						

DAY 18

Read each pair of sentences. Circle the word in the first sentence that is the antonym for the bold word in the second sentence.

8. The air was moist and cool after the heavy rain last night.

   Once the sun was out for a couple of hours, the air seemed to be **dry**.

9. A lost dog was enclosed in a pen until the owner came to get her.

   When the dog was **released** to her owner, she jumped up to lick him.

10. Dad was ignorant about the driving laws when he visited England.

    He quickly became **knowledgeable** by reading a book of the rules.

11. Dripping water from our roof will freeze in the winter and make icicles.

    Sometimes, it is spring before the icicles **thaw** and disappear.

12. Madame Proctor purchased a valuable diamond at the auction.

    The diamond turned out to be **worthless** when she discovered that it was fake.

Write a word or group of words from the word bank to complete each sentence.

| center of Earth | core | inner core |
| lithosphere | mantle | outer core |

13. The core of Earth has two parts. The _____ is liquid.

    The _____ is solid.

14. One reason that the crust and upper _____

    are brittle is because they are the outermost and coldest layers of Earth.

15. The _____ includes the crust and the uppermost mantle.

16. The _____ is the thickest layer and is extremely hot.

17. As the _____ is approached, pressure and

    temperature increase.

FACTOID: Astronauts clean dishes using wet and dry wipes.

Add or subtract. Write answers in simplest form.

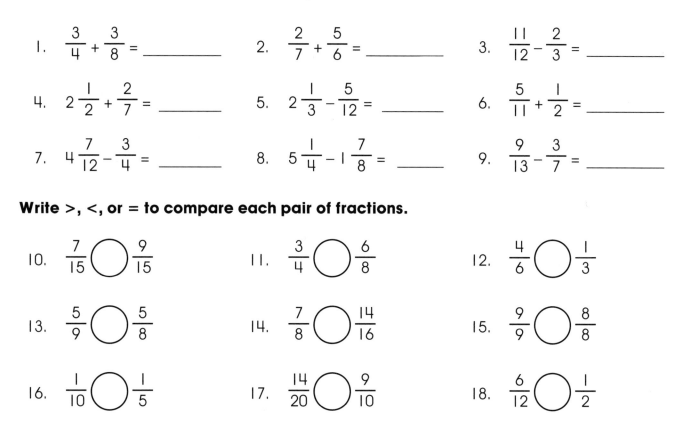

1. $\dfrac{3}{4} + \dfrac{3}{8} =$ _____

2. $\dfrac{2}{7} + \dfrac{5}{6} =$ _____

3. $\dfrac{11}{12} - \dfrac{2}{3} =$ _____

4. $2\dfrac{1}{2} + \dfrac{2}{7} =$ _____

5. $2\dfrac{1}{3} - \dfrac{5}{12} =$ _____

6. $\dfrac{5}{11} + \dfrac{1}{2} =$ _____

7. $4\dfrac{7}{12} - \dfrac{3}{4} =$ _____

8. $5\dfrac{1}{4} - 1\dfrac{7}{8} =$ _____

9. $\dfrac{9}{13} - \dfrac{3}{7} =$ _____

Write >, <, or = to compare each pair of fractions.

10. $\dfrac{7}{15} \bigcirc \dfrac{9}{15}$

11. $\dfrac{3}{4} \bigcirc \dfrac{6}{8}$

12. $\dfrac{4}{6} \bigcirc \dfrac{1}{3}$

13. $\dfrac{5}{9} \bigcirc \dfrac{5}{8}$

14. $\dfrac{7}{8} \bigcirc \dfrac{14}{16}$

15. $\dfrac{9}{9} \bigcirc \dfrac{8}{8}$

16. $\dfrac{1}{10} \bigcirc \dfrac{1}{5}$

17. $\dfrac{14}{20} \bigcirc \dfrac{9}{10}$

18. $\dfrac{6}{12} \bigcirc \dfrac{1}{2}$

Underline the complete perfect-tense verb in each sentence.

19. George had explained the plot of the movie to his brother.

20. Oliver had tried all the flavors of yogurt made by Yummy-Yo.

21. Zara has visited her grandma in Toronto twice this year.

22. By Thursday, the Desmonds will have returned from vacation.

23. Alice has been excited about the school dance all day.

24. Rachel will have played piano for six years this June.

25. Roberto had hoped the storm would pass before the game.

26. I will have read all the books on the top shelf by the end of the month.

DAY 19

Read the passage. Then, answer the questions.

Ancient Greece

The people of Ancient Greece lived nearly 4,000 years ago. They created beautiful buildings, and they held the first Olympic Games. The original Olympics were held every four years for more than 1,000 years. The Greeks also came up with the idea of democracy, or government by the people rather than government by a single ruler. The Greeks created small figurines and life-sized statues. They built public buildings, like theaters and stadiums. Modern sports arenas are still based on ancient Greek stadiums.

The Ancient Greeks made many contributions to science, mathematics, and medicine. Greek medical texts were used for hundreds of years. Because Greece is made up of several islands, many Greeks were fishermen and sailors. They established trade routes throughout the ancient world. The Greek poet Homer wrote two epic poems that are still read today. *The Iliad* and *The Odyssey* told the stories of heroes who traveled the world.

27. What is the main idea of this passage?
    A. The ancient Greeks had many accomplishments in art, science, and sports.
    B. The ancient Greeks lived nearly 4,000 years ago.
    C. The ancient Greeks held the first Olympic Games.

28. Name three accomplishments of the ancient Greeks. _____

    _____

    _____

29. What is one way that Greek architecture influenced modern buildings?

    _____

    _____

30. How does the author support the topic sentence in paragraph 2? _____

    _____

31. How can you tell that the Greeks' accomplishments in medicine were admired?

    _____

FITNESS FLASH: Do 10 shoulder shrugs.

* See page ii.

Write each equivalent fraction.

1. $\dfrac{3}{4} = \dfrac{}{8}$

2. $\dfrac{5}{8} = \dfrac{}{16}$

3. $\dfrac{10}{25} = \dfrac{2}{}$

4. $\dfrac{4}{9} = \dfrac{}{36}$

5. $\dfrac{7}{12} = \dfrac{28}{}$

6. $\dfrac{6}{6} = \dfrac{12}{}$

7. $\dfrac{3}{4} = \dfrac{}{20}$

8. $\dfrac{7}{15} = \dfrac{}{45}$

9. $\dfrac{9}{12} = \dfrac{36}{}$

10. $\dfrac{2}{3} = \dfrac{10}{}$

11. $\dfrac{3}{10} = \dfrac{18}{}$

12. $\dfrac{1}{3} = \dfrac{3}{}$

13. $\dfrac{5}{8} = \dfrac{}{72}$

14. $\dfrac{2}{5} = \dfrac{8}{}$

15. $\dfrac{5}{12} = \dfrac{}{36}$

16. $\dfrac{11}{24} = \dfrac{44}{}$

Each sentence is missing a comma. Use this proofreading mark to add each comma needed: ⌃.

17. Meanwhile Mom and Dad wrapped Diego's gifts.

18. After the storm had blown over Grandpa went outside to survey the damage.

19. You haven't locked your keys in the car have you?

20. Yes I think the outfit you're wearing is appropriate for the recital.

21. Furthermore you didn't do any of your chores this week.

22. Did you remember to lock the back door Danny?

23. Next mix the milk, oil, and egg into the dry ingredients.

24. Dr. Alonzo have you received the results of the tests yet?

25. On Wednesday morning Tara has an orthodontist appointment.

26. Although Liam was pleased with the final results of his art project he had struggled a bit in the beginning.

27. Mrs. Antonelli doesn't know the Rockwell twins does she?

DAY 20

Read each pair of sentences. Circle the word in the first sentence that is the antonym for the bold word in the second sentence.

28. Ben enjoys Saturdays because he goes to his grandparents' farm.

    He **dislikes** when it is time to leave them and their farm animals.

29. Hurricanes and tornadoes can destroy anything in their paths.

    Sometimes, it takes months to **repair** the damage they cause.

30. When Nancy is at the park, she often plays on the swings.

    She **seldom** has to wait to take her turn.

31. It was foolish of Ricky not to study for the science test.

    When he saw his grade, he wished that he had been more **sensible** and had studied for it.

32. When Cathy woke, she had to face reality.

    She realized that her dreams the night before were just **fantasy**.

Round each number to the nearest tenth.

33. 5.684 _____

34. 0.374 _____

35. 2.415 _____

36. 3.012 _____

37. 8.542 _____

38. 0.894 _____

39. 5.975 _____

40. 6.014 _____

Round each number to the nearest hundredth.

41. 2.154 _____

42. 0.947 _____

43. 3.249 _____

44. 9.893 _____

45. 7.109 _____

46. 5.005 _____

47. 1.251 _____

48. 2.457 _____

CHARACTER CHECK: During the day, watch for people who are demonstrating kindness. At the end of the day, share with a family member the kindness you observed.

Growing Crystals

Have you ever looked closely at ice crystals? What about salt crystals? In this activity, you can grow all kinds of crystals yourself!

Materials
- 10 tsp. water
- 5 tsp. salt
- 5 tsp. laundry bluing
- 1 tsp. ammonia
- food coloring
- charcoal briquettes
- pie pan
- teaspoon
- bowl

Procedure
1. With an adult, mix the water, salt, laundry bluing, and ammonia in a bowl.
2. Place the charcoal pieces in the pie pan. Pour just enough of the solution over the charcoal so that it covers the bottom of the pan.
3. To make colorful crystals, drizzle the food coloring over the top of the pile of charcoal. Or, to make white crystals with a blue tint, do not use any food coloring.
4. Crystals will begin to form right away on the charcoal and in the pan. As the solution evaporates, add more to the pan. Caution: If you pour the solution directly on the charcoal, the crystals, which are very fragile, will be crushed. Even blowing very hard on the crystals will knock them over.

What's This All About?
Charcoal is a porous material. It absorbs the liquid in the bottom of the pie pan, and the liquid that is poured over it evaporates, leaving a crystal garden. The garden will continue to grow until the pan runs out of the solution or until the crystals grow too tall to support their own weight and fall.

Take a picture of the results of your experiment. Write a letter or an e-mail to a friend or relative and include the photo. Explain the steps of the experiment as well as the process that occurred to create the crystals.

BONUS

Air Pressure

How does the carbon dioxide in Earth's atmosphere affect the air temperature?

Materials
- 2 aquarium thermometers
- ruler
- tape
- 2 clear plastic storage containers with lids
- water
- 2 effervescent antacid and pain reliever tablets
- 2 identical lamps with 200-watt bulbs

Procedure

1. Place the aquarium thermometers approximately 1 inch (2.5 cm) below the opening of the plastic storage containers so that they can be read from the outside. Tape the thermometers in place.

2. Add water to each plastic storage container to a depth of approximately 1.5 inches (3.8 cm). Place the lid on each container.

3. Lift the lid on one container slightly and quickly drop in two effervescent antacid and pain reliever tablets. The tablets will react with the water to produce carbon dioxide gas. Close the lid quickly to trap the carbon dioxide gas within the "atmosphere" of the container. Label the container.

4. Place one lamp above each container. The distance and location of the lamp above each container should be identical.

5. Take a temperature reading every 10 minutes until three consecutive readings are the same for each container. Record your readings in a graph.

What's This All About?

Burning fossil fuels to obtain energy creates chemical by-products that are dangerous in the atmosphere. Carbon dioxide, a greenhouse gas, is one chemical by-product that concerns many scientists. They think that the increase of carbon dioxide in the atmosphere is affecting the planet's temperatures. The carbon dioxide in the atmosphere absorbs solar energy and traps excess heat. Within this century, carbon dioxide levels have risen, as have global temperatures.

There are two opposing views concerning global warming: one is that the warming is part of Earth's natural cycle, and the other is that human activities are increasing global temperatures.

44

The 50 States

Label as many U.S. states as you can. Use an atlas to finish if you need help.

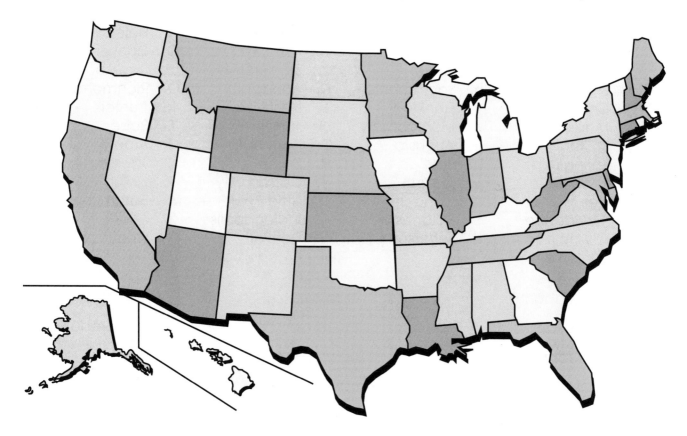

Alabama (AL)	Alaska (AK)	Arizona (AZ)	Arkansas (AR)
California (CA)	Colorado (CO)	Connecticut (CT)	Delaware (DE)
Florida (FL)	Georgia (GA)	Hawaii (HI)	Idaho (ID)
Illinois (IL)	Indiana (IN)	Iowa (IA)	Kansas (KS)
Kentucky (KY)	Louisiana (LA)	Maine (ME)	Maryland (MD)
Massachusetts (MA)	Michigan (MI)	Minnesota (MN)	Mississippi (MS)
Missouri (MO)	Montana (MT)	Nebraska (NE)	Nevada (NV)
New Hampshire (NH)	New Jersey (NJ)	New Mexico (NM)	New York (NY)
North Carolina (NC)	North Dakota (ND)	Ohio (OH)	Oklahoma (OK)
Oregon (OR)	Pennsylvania (PA)	Rhode Island (RI)	South Carolina (SC)
South Dakota (SD)	Tennessee (TN)	Texas (TX)	Utah (UT)
Vermont (VT)	Virginia (VA)	Washington (WA)	West Virginia (WV)
Wisconsin (WI)	Wyoming (WY)		

BONUS

U.S. States and Capitals

Match each U.S. state with the correct capital.

a. Montpelier	n. Salem	A. Salt Lake City	N. Helena
b. Honolulu	o. Boston	B. Lansing	O. Cheyenne
c. Hartford	p. Pierre	C. Bismarck	P. Topeka
d. Lincoln	q. Sacramento	D. Annapolis	Q. Richmond
e. Columbus	r. Frankfort	E. Nashville	R. Trenton
f. Madison	s. Montgomery	F. Juneau	S. Boise
g. St. Paul	t. Augusta	G. Harrisburg	T. Albany
h. Springfield	u. Raleigh	H. Dover	U. Jackson
i. Phoenix	v. Austin	I. Carson City	V. Columbia
j. Des Moines	w. Concord	J. Little Rock	W. Baton Rouge
k. Providence	x. Tallahassee	K. Indianapolis	X. Atlanta
l. Olympia	y. Jefferson City	L. Denver	Y. Charleston
m. Santa Fe		M. Oklahoma City	

1. ____ Alabama
2. ____ Alaska
3. ____ Arizona

4. ____ Arkansas
5. ____ California
6. ____ Colorado

7. ____ Connecticut
8. ____ Delaware
9. ____ Florida

10. ____ Georgia
11. ____ Hawaii
12. ____ Idaho

13. ____ Illinois
14. ____ Indiana
15. ____ Iowa

16. ____ Kansas
17. ____ Kentucky
18. ____ Louisiana

19. ____ Maine
20. ____ Maryland
21. ____ Massachusetts

22. ____ Michigan
23. ____ Minnesota
24. ____ Mississippi

25. ____ Missouri
26. ____ Montana
27. ____ Nebraska

28. ____ Nevada
29. ____ New Hampshire
30. ____ New Jersey

31. ____ New Mexico
32. ____ New York
33. ____ North Carolina

34. ____ North Dakota
35. ____ Ohio
36. ____ Oklahoma

37. ____ Oregon
38. ____ Pennsylvania
39. ____ Rhode Island

40. ____ South Carolina
41. ____ South Dakota
42. ____ Tennessee

43. ____ Texas
44. ____ Utah
45. ____ Vermont

46. ____ Virginia
47. ____ Washington
48. ____ West Virginia

49. ____ Wisconsin
50. ____ Wyoming

Where I Live

Draw the shape of your state or province and label where you live. Draw your state or province's flower and bird.

BONUS

Take It Outside!

Summer is the perfect time to plan a family day trip to your state or province's capital. With an adult, discuss some of the places that you would like to visit. Talk with friends and neighbors who have visited the capital and get their recommendations. Make a list of the places you decide you would like to see in your state or province's capital. Check online to gather information about guided tours of these places, their hours of operation, and their admission prices. Write a proposal and present it to your family, encouraging them to place this day trip on the family's summer calendar.

With an adult, take a bike ride or nature walk around your neighborhood. Your goal is to look for samples of compound words. Be sure to bring a pen and a notebook. Every now and then, stop at a safe spot, record some of what you have seen, and list the compound words that you have discovered, such as *ladybug, firefly,* and *sunflower.* When you return home, write a poem or short story using at least two of the compound words that you discovered on your outdoor excursion.

Summer is an especially good time for a cookout. Schedule a cookout and invite your family, friends, and neighbors to attend. Plan a menu that includes a choice of items for an adult to grill, such as chicken, hamburgers, and veggie burgers. Poll your neighbors before the cookout. The poll will help you determine the amount of food to purchase. Prior to the barbecue, make a bar graph to display near the grill, enabling people to see the neighborhood preferences.

* See page ii.

Monthly Goals

Think of three goals to set for yourself this month. For example, you may want to read for 30 minutes each day. Write your goals on the lines. Post them someplace visible, where you will see them every day.

Draw a line through each goal as you meet it. Feel proud that you have met your goal, and set new ones to continue to challenge yourself.

1. _____

2. _____

3. _____

Word List

The following words are used in this section. Use a dictionary to look up each word that you do not know. Then, write three sentences. Use a word from the word list in each sentence.

align	increment
archaeologists	integrity
ecosystem	lunges
elaborate	manor
epicenter	tiers

1. _____

_____

2. _____

_____

3. _____

_____

Introduction to Strength

This section includes fitness and character development activities that focus on strength. These activities are designed to get you moving and thinking about strengthening your body and your character.

Physical Strength

Like flexibility, strength is important for a healthy body. Many people think that a strong person is someone who can lift an enormous amount of weight. However, strength is more than the ability to pick up heavy barbells. Having strength is important for many everyday activities, such as helping with yardwork or helping a younger sibling get into a car. Muscular strength also helps reduce stress on your joints as your body ages.

Everyday activities and many fun exercises provide opportunities for you to build strength. Carrying bags of groceries, riding a bicycle, and swimming are all excellent ways to strengthen your muscles. Classic exercises, such as push-ups and chin-ups, are also fantastic strength-builders.

Set realistic, achievable goals to improve your strength based on the activities that you enjoy. Evaluate your progress during the summer months and set new strength goals for yourself as you accomplish your previous goals.

Strength of Character

As you build your physical strength, work on your inner strength as well. Having a strong character means standing up for your beliefs, even if others do not agree with your viewpoint. Inner strength can be shown in many ways. For example, you can show inner strength by being honest, standing up for someone who needs your help, and putting your best effort into every task. It is not always easy to show inner strength. Think of a time when you showed inner strength, such as telling the truth when you broke your mother's favorite vase. How did you use your inner strength to handle that situation?

Use the summer months to develop a strong sense of self, both physically and emotionally. Celebrate your successes and look for ways to become even stronger. Reflect upon your accomplishments during the summer, and you will see positive growth on the inside and on the outside.

Change each fraction into an equivalent mixed number.

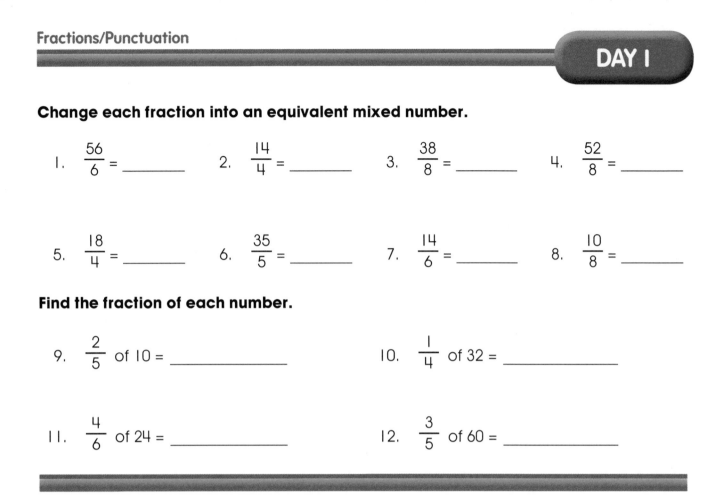

1. $\dfrac{56}{6} = $ _____

2. $\dfrac{14}{4} = $ _____

3. $\dfrac{38}{8} = $ _____

4. $\dfrac{52}{8} = $ _____

5. $\dfrac{18}{4} = $ _____

6. $\dfrac{35}{5} = $ _____

7. $\dfrac{14}{6} = $ _____

8. $\dfrac{10}{8} = $ _____

Find the fraction of each number.

9. $\dfrac{2}{5}$ of 10 = _____

10. $\dfrac{1}{4}$ of 32 = _____

11. $\dfrac{4}{6}$ of 24 = _____

12. $\dfrac{3}{5}$ of 60 = _____

Are the commas in each sentence used correctly? Write *yes* or *no*.

13. The Smiths visited Philadelphia, Pennsylvania and New, York. _____

14. They saw museums, of art, history and science in Philadelphia. _____

15. Don, Debbie, and Dan toured Independence Hall. _____

Write commas where they are needed in each sentence.

16. Debbie Don and Dan were impressed with New York City.

17. It is an important business cultural and trade center.

18. The Bronx Manhattan Queens Brooklyn and Staten Island are its five boroughs.

19. Chinatown Greenwich Village and Harlem are three neighborhoods in Manhattan.

20. The Smiths saw Times Square Rockefeller Center and the United Nations Headquarters.

DAY I

Write a synonym for each word.

21. jump _____

22. crawl _____

23. quickly _____

24. tired _____

25. sprint _____

Write an antonym for each word.

26. narrow _____

27. near _____

28. horrible _____

29. open _____

30. find _____

Read the passage. Then, answer the questions.

Earth is like a huge magnet. It has a magnetic field. Its magnetism is the strongest at the north and south poles. When a rock forms, magnetic particles within the rock align themselves with Earth's magnetic field. They will point toward either the north or south pole. There are some rocks that do not point to the current north and south poles. Scientists conclude that either the north and south poles have moved, or the rocks themselves have moved since they first formed. Most scientists think that the rocks and continents have moved. Geologists use this information to determine how the continents have moved over time.

31. Why is Earth compared to a magnet? _____

32. Where are Earth's strongest points of magnetism? _____

33. How can geologists study the movements of the continents? _____

_____

FACTOID: There are 750,000 known kinds of insects.

To multiply fractions, first multiply the numerators. Then, multiply the denominators. When you multiply two fractions, the product is smaller than the two factors. Find each product. Simplify each fraction. Then, draw a fraction picture to illustrate each answer.

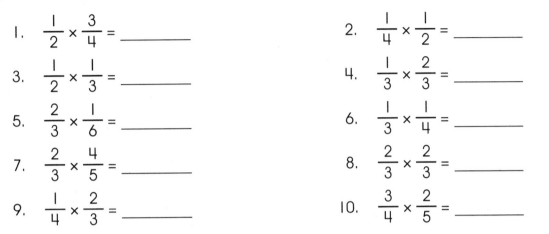

1. $\dfrac{1}{2} \times \dfrac{3}{4} =$ _____

2. $\dfrac{1}{4} \times \dfrac{1}{2} =$ _____

3. $\dfrac{1}{2} \times \dfrac{1}{3} =$ _____

4. $\dfrac{1}{3} \times \dfrac{2}{3} =$ _____

5. $\dfrac{2}{3} \times \dfrac{1}{6} =$ _____

6. $\dfrac{1}{3} \times \dfrac{1}{4} =$ _____

7. $\dfrac{2}{3} \times \dfrac{4}{5} =$ _____

8. $\dfrac{2}{3} \times \dfrac{2}{3} =$ _____

9. $\dfrac{1}{4} \times \dfrac{2}{3} =$ _____

10. $\dfrac{3}{4} \times \dfrac{2}{5} =$ _____

Complete each sentence with a word from the word bank.

however	nevertheless	moreover
although	similarly	in addition

11. Mr. Oh was supposed to pick up Susan at 4:00. _____, the heavy traffic caused him to be 15 minutes late.

12. _____ it hasn't rained in almost two weeks, our vegetable garden is doing well.

13. Gabriela has six chickens _____ to a dog, a rabbit, three cats, and a goldfish.

14. The weather for our picnic was a bit soggy, but the day was fun

_____.

15. *To Kill a Mockingbird* is a classic American novel. _____, it's a very moving story.

16. A female kangaroo carries her baby in her pouch for about nine months.

_____, a mother wombat carries her baby in her pouch for the first half year of its life.

Read the passage. Then, answer the questions.

The Mayan Empire

The Maya lived in Central America from about 2600 BC to about AD 900. The Mayan Empire covered present-day Guatemala, Belize, and El Salvador, as well as part of Honduras and southeastern Mexico. The Maya built elaborate stone temples, palaces, and buildings called *observatories* from which they could watch the movements of the planets and stars. They created a calendar with 260 days to mark special days in their civilization. Every 20th day, the Maya held a festival.

The Mayan ruins in Chichén Itzá, Mexico, include performance stages, markets, and even a ball court. Many Mayan foods are still eaten in Central America, including maize (corn), beans, chili peppers, and squash. The Maya wore beautiful woven fabrics, feathered headdresses, and hats. No one is sure why the Maya disappeared, but archaeologists hope to find out.

17. What is the main idea of this passage?

   A.   The Maya built many great buildings.

   B.   The Maya suddenly disappeared.

   C.   The Maya lived in Central America thousands of years ago.

18. How long did the Maya live in Central America? _____

_____

19. Which modern countries did the Mayan Empire cover? _____

_____

20. What was special about the Mayan calendar? _____

_____

_____

21. Reread the last sentence of the passage. What purpose does it serve? Is it an

   effective ending for the passage? Why or why not? _____

_____

_____

FITNESS FLASH: Do 10 lunges.

* See page ii.

Find each product. Simplify each fraction.

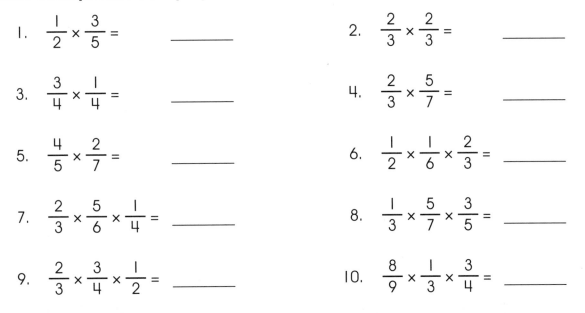

1. $\frac{1}{2} \times \frac{3}{5} =$ _____

2. $\frac{2}{3} \times \frac{2}{3} =$ _____

3. $\frac{3}{4} \times \frac{1}{4} =$ _____

4. $\frac{2}{3} \times \frac{5}{7} =$ _____

5. $\frac{4}{5} \times \frac{2}{7} =$ _____

6. $\frac{1}{2} \times \frac{1}{6} \times \frac{2}{3} =$ _____

7. $\frac{2}{3} \times \frac{5}{6} \times \frac{1}{4} =$ _____

8. $\frac{1}{3} \times \frac{5}{7} \times \frac{3}{5} =$ _____

9. $\frac{2}{3} \times \frac{3}{4} \times \frac{1}{2} =$ _____

10. $\frac{8}{9} \times \frac{1}{3} \times \frac{3}{4} =$ _____

Replace each underlined word with a preposition from the word bank to show a different relationship between the words in each sentence.

behind	near	through	under	until

EXAMPLE: Grayson found his backpack ~~under~~ __**near**__ his desk.

11. Julie stood <u>beside</u> _____ me at the parade.

12. Did you leave this box <u>on</u> _____ the bench?

13. The children will play <u>after</u> _____ dark.

14. The bats flew <u>into</u> _____ the window.

The object of the preposition is the noun or pronoun following a preposition. Write an object (noun or pronoun) for each underlined preposition.

15. That boy had a glass <u>of</u> _____ .

16. We climbed <u>over</u> a _____ .

17. Jayla fell <u>off</u> her _____ .

18. Far <u>below</u> the _____ , we could see the river.

DAY 3

Write the homophone in parentheses that matches each definition. Use a dictionary if you need help.

19. _____ : grinds or crushes with the teeth (chews, choose)

20. _____ : inexpensive; of little value (cheap, cheep)

21. _____ : a large mammal with long shaggy fur (bare, bear)

22. _____ : having little or no color; not bright (pail, pale)

23. _____ : a house on a large estate (manner, manor)

24. _____ : a series of rows, one above another (tears, tiers)

25. _____ : a long, slender object usually shaped like a cylinder (pole, poll)

26. _____ : something to be learned (lessen, lesson)

Use the time line to answer each question about the events leading up to the Revolutionary War.

1754	1763	1765	1770	1773	1774	1775
French and Indian War	King George III limits Western settlement	Stamp Act	Boston Massacre	Boston Tea Party	Intolerable Acts	Battles fought at Lexington and Concord

27. How many years after the French and Indian War did the Boston

    Massacre occur? _____

28. Which events occurred in Boston? _____

    _____

29. Which occurred first—the Stamp Act or the Intolerable Acts? How many years

    were between these events? _____

30. Who gave a proclamation to limit Western settlement? _____

31. Where were the battles fought in 1775? _____

FACTOID: There are 88 keys on a standard piano.

Match each term with its definition.

1. _____ fraction

A. the answer you get when you divide one number by another number

2. _____ improper fraction

B. the number found below the line in a fraction

3. _____ quotient

C. a number that names a part of a set or whole

4. _____ mixed number

D. the number found above the line in a fraction

5. _____ denominator

E. a number that has a whole number and a fraction

6. _____ numerator

F. a fraction whose numerator is greater than or equal to its denominator

Fill in each blank.

7. Write $2 \div 9$ as a fraction. _____

8. Write $15 \div 7$ as an improper fraction.

_____

9. $82 \div 7$ can be written _____ or $7\overline{)82}$.

What is the divisor? _____

What is the remainder? _____

Write it as a mixed number. _____

10. What kind of fractions are $\dfrac{28}{5}$ and $\dfrac{59}{7}$? _____

Write a mixed number for each fraction. _____

A *prepositional phrase* is made up of a preposition and its object. **Underline each prepositional phrase.**

EXAMPLE: around the playground

11. between the bases	12. along the trail	13. until four o'clock
14. near the window	15. the circus elephant	16. the math problem
17. a hanging light	18. outside the door	19. are the bridges
20. the wet streets	21. under the house	22. in the barn
23. things that have gills	24. your guide	25. how you will be

DAY 4

Circle the correct homophone(s) to complete each sentence.

26. Tanya (new, knew) how to get along with (new, knew) people.

27. The (our, hour) hand on (our, hour) new clock does not move correctly.

28. I like to (read, reed) magazines about sports.

29. You can (buy, by) a good used TV in the store next (to, two, too) the shopping mall.

30. Spencer and Jack invited me to come to (there, their) house after school.

31. Mrs. Brinks told her students to bring (to, two, too) pencils to class for the test.

32. I (see, sea) a beautiful sunset down by the (see, sea) every night.

33. Our cat, Cosby, sometimes chases his (tale, tail).

Strength in Numbers!

Find a pair of dice and get ready to become stronger! Study the list of activities below. Roll the dice and add the numbers shown. Then, choose one of the activities and do the same number of repetitions as the sum from the dice. For example, if you rolled a seven, you might choose to do seven jumping jacks. Write the number of repetitions beside each exercise. You must complete each exercise once, and no exercise can be repeated during a round. Repeat rounds of exercises to match your fitness level.

Exercise	Repetitions	Repetitions	Repetitions	Repetitions	Repetitions
push-ups					
sit-ups					
jumping jacks					
arm circles					
hopping on one leg					
lunges					
leg lifts					

FITNESS FLASH: Do 10 squats.

* See page ii.

To divide fractions, multiply the first fraction by the reciprocal of the divisor. Find each quotient. Simplify each fraction.

EXAMPLE: $\dfrac{2}{3} \div \dfrac{4}{5} =$

$$\dfrac{2}{3} \times \dfrac{5}{4} = \dfrac{10}{12} = \dfrac{5}{6}$$

1. $\dfrac{5}{8} \div \dfrac{2}{6} =$ _____

2. $\dfrac{3}{4} \div \dfrac{1}{2} =$ _____

3. $\dfrac{1}{5} \div \dfrac{3}{10} =$ _____

4. $\dfrac{1}{6} \div \dfrac{1}{12} =$ _____

5. $\dfrac{4}{5} \div \dfrac{2}{3} =$ _____

6. $\dfrac{2}{8} \div \dfrac{3}{4} =$ _____

7. $\dfrac{6}{7} \div \dfrac{8}{12} =$ _____

8. $\dfrac{1}{5} \div \dfrac{1}{2} =$ _____

9. $\dfrac{9}{12} \div \dfrac{8}{10} =$ _____

10. $\dfrac{3}{4} \div \dfrac{1}{7} =$ _____

11. $\dfrac{7}{9} \div \dfrac{2}{6} =$ _____

12. $\dfrac{4}{9} \div \dfrac{2}{5} =$ _____

Write *and*, *or*, or *but* to complete each sentence.

13. Jenna _____ Lamont are on the same baseball team.

14. She wanted the team color to be blue, _____ he preferred red.

15. The players chose their favorite positions, _____ they were very pleased.

16. Jenna plays either first base _____ in the outfield.

17. In the first inning, Jenna hit a single, _____ Lamont hit a double.

18. Their team was winning, _____ the other team caught up in the fourth inning.

19. Jenna stopped one runner, _____ Lamont let the other runner get to third base.

20. Their team scored three more runs, _____ the score was tied.

DAY 5

Read the passage. Then, answer the questions.

Harriet Tubman

Harriet Tubman used the Underground Railroad, a secret system of safe houses and people, to escape from slavery. Tubman went to Philadelphia, Pennsylvania, where she could live as a free person. Escaping from slavery was hard and dangerous. But, Tubman was brave, and once she was free, she wanted to help others become free too. She returned to the South and helped her family members and other slaves escape. Harriet Tubman worked on the Underground Railroad from 1850 to 1860.

When the Civil War started, Tubman became a spy. Many women worked as spies during the war, but few took as many risks as Tubman did. Tubman knew the land in the South, and she knew ways to travel without being caught. She gathered information to help the Northern army. Tubman even led a group of African American soldiers on a raid. The group freed more than 700 slaves. No woman had led American soldiers on a raid before. Tubman also worked as a nurse. She cared for wounded African American soldiers and slaves. After the war, Tubman helped the freed slaves. She opened her home to take care of the elderly, and she worked for women's rights. Harriet Tubman was one of the strongest and bravest women in American history.

21. What is the main idea of this passage?
    A. Harriet Tubman was a strong woman.
    B. Harriet Tubman was a slave who escaped.
    C. Harriet Tubman was a strong woman who spent her life helping others.

22. Number the events in the order they happened.

    _____ Tubman worked for women's rights.

    _____ Tubman escaped to freedom in the North.

    _____ Tubman worked as a spy.

    _____ Tubman's work helping slaves escape ended when the war started.

23. What did Tubman do during the war that no other woman had ever done?

    _____

24. Name something Tubman did after the war. _____

25. Describe the author's point of view. How does he or she feel about Harriet

    Tubman? How do you know? _____

    _____

When adding or subtracting decimals, first line up the decimals. If the amount of decimal places in the numbers is not the same, add zeros to the end of the number with fewer decimal places. Solve each problem.

EXAMPLE: 3.45 + 5.923 = **3.450**
$$\begin{array}{r} \textbf{3.450} \\ +\ \textbf{5.923} \\ \hline \textbf{9.373} \end{array}$$

1. 18.91 + 11.5 = _____

2. 34.09 – 9.407 = _____

3. 3.806 + 5.29 = _____

4. 185.04 – 165.9 = _____

5. 437.7 + 13.906 = _____

6. 379.76 – 37.435 = _____

7. 42.881 + 8.96 = _____

8. $224.00 – $116.98 = _____

Write an interjection from the word bank on each line. Use an exclamation point to show strong emotion. Use a comma to show weaker emotion.

Great	Hey	Oh	Oh no	Phew	Wow	Yes

9. _____ why is the classroom so busy today?

10. _____ I forgot that we are pretending to build a pyramid.

11. _____ It looks like ancient Egypt!

12. _____ We tried to decorate in an ancient style.

13. _____ Millie remembered to wear her costume.

14. _____ I almost forgot to bring mine!

15. _____ I remembered that it was in my backpack!

DAY 6

Multiply or divide by powers of ten. Look at each answer. Is the number of zeros correct? Did you place the decimal point correctly?

16. $19 \times 10^5 =$ _____

17. $.652 \div 10^3 =$ _____

18. $.54 \times 10^8 =$ _____

19. $201 \times 10^2 =$ _____

20. $80{,}000 \times 10^3 =$ _____

21. $.714 \times 10^4 =$ _____

22. $.2 \div 10^6 =$ _____

23. $.857 \times 10^1 =$ _____

24. $75 \times 10^9 =$ _____

25. $1.52 \times 10^4 =$ _____

26. $50 \times 10^5 =$ _____

27. $235.48 \div 10^2 =$ _____

28. $8.951 \times 10^7 =$ _____

29. $700 \times 10^3 =$ _____

30. $125.98 \times 10^8 =$ _____

You have just learned that you will share a bedroom with a younger brother or sister. Write a letter explaining to your family why you feel that this is or is not a good idea.

_____

_____

_____

_____

_____

_____

_____

_____

_____

FACTOID: Approximately one million Earths could fit inside the sun.

Fill in the table with information from the passage and answer the question.

Amanda opened a checking account on May 15 with $500.25. On May 31, she deposited $496.80. On June 4, she withdrew $145.00 to buy a bicycle. On June 15, she deposited $435.20. On June 30, she deposited $600.00. On July 1, she withdrew $463.00 to buy a sleeping bag and pay for camp. On July 15, she deposited $110.00. On July 24, she withdrew $600.00 to buy a computer.

Date	Deposit	Withdrawal	Total $
May 15	$500.25		$500.25
May 31			
June 4			
June 15			
June 30			
July 1			
July 15			
July 24			

One word in each set is spelled incorrectly. Underline the misspelled word and write the correct spelling on the line. You may use a dictionary if needed.

1. joyous   genre   iceburg   _____

2. hatchet   symmetry   sieze   _____

3. commitee   exterior   regret   _____

4. drowsy   oblige   demacratic   _____

5. mythical   quotasion   scenario   _____

6. destination   slugish   excel   _____

7. attire   opress   grievance   _____

8. plack   adopt   bankrupt   _____

CHARACTER CHECK: Make a list of at least five ways that you can show respect at home and at school. Share the list with a family member.

DAY 7

An *analogy* shows a relationship between two sets of words or phrases. Complete each analogy.

EXAMPLE: *Preview* is to *previewed* as *decide* is to _____decided_____ .

9. *Hear* is to *ear* as *talk* is to _____ .

10. *Griddle* is to *pancake* as *pot* is to _____ .

11. *Author* is to *book* as *artist* is to _____ .

12. *Business* is to *businesses* as *address* is to _____ .

13. *Research* is to *researcher* as *garden* is to _____ .

14. *Breakfast* is to *lunch* as *morning* is to _____ .

15. *Control* is to *controllable* as *reason* is to _____ .

16. *TV* is to *commercial* as *magazine* is to _____ .

17. *Manager* is to *store* as *principal* is to _____ .

Think of something you know how to do well. You may know how to knit, play basketball, ride a skateboard, create a Web page, or care for a hamster. Share your knowledge by writing a paragraph that explains how to do something, step by step. If you need more information, you can do research online or at the library.

_____

_____

_____

_____

_____

_____

_____

_____

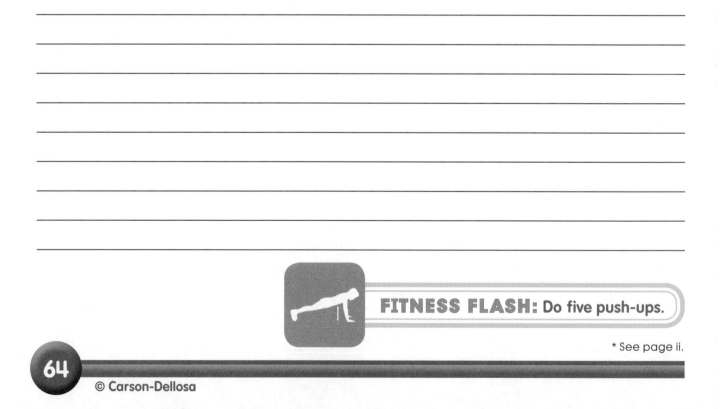

FITNESS FLASH: Do five push-ups.

* See page ii.

Find each product. Add extra zeros when necessary.

1.   41.5
    × 0.17

2.   1.09
    × 0.68

3.   3.05
    × 85.2

4.   0.003
    ×   3.9

5.   7.4
    × 0.07

6.   0.09
    × 2.3

7.   0.035
    × 0.02

8.   0.005
    ×   55

Decide what type of figurative language appears in each sentence. On the line, write *S* for simile, *M* for metaphor, *H* for hyperbole, or *P* for personification.

9. _____ The surface of the frozen lake glistened like glass as the sun set.

10. _____ At dawn, two small birds outside my window demanded that I get up immediately.

11. _____ I have asked you a million times to pick up your wet towels!

12. _____ The tornado was a train coming full speed at the town.

13. _____ Silas's hair was as shiny as a new copper penny.

14. _____ It's going to take me a hundred years to clean up this room.

15. _____ The sunflowers lifted their heavy heads and smiled at the late morning sun.

16. _____ Devon is a real tiger when he has his mind set on something.

CHARACTER CHECK: Draw a comic strip showing a character who demonstrates loyalty.

DAY 8

Read the passage. Then, answer the questions.

Wild Geese by Celia Thaxter

The wild wind blows, the sun shines, the birds sing loud,
The blue, blue sky is flecked with fleecy dappled cloud,
Over earth's rejoicing fields the children dance and sing,
And the frogs pipe in chorus, "It is spring! It is spring!"

The grass comes, the flower laughs where lately lay the snow,
O'er the breezy hill-top hoarsely calls the crow,
By the flowing river the alder catkins swing,
And the sweet song-sparrow cries, "Spring! It is spring!"

Hark, what a clamor goes winging through the sky!
Look, children! Listen to the sound so wild and high!
Like a **peal** of broken bells,—kling, klang, kling,—
Far and high the wild geese cry, "Spring! It is spring!"

Bear the winter off with you, O wild geese dear!
Carry all the cold away, far away from here;
Chase the snow into the north, O strong of heart and wing,
While we share the robin's rapture, crying "Spring! It is spring!"

17. Give one example of personification from the poem. _____
    _____

18. In the third line of the third stanza, what does *peal* mean? _____
    _____

19. How does the poet feel about the coming of spring? Support your answer with
    details from the poem. _____
    _____
    _____
    _____
    _____

FACTOID: There are approximately 50 million penguins in Antarctica.

Find each product.

1.	0.12	2.	0.08	3.	4.6	4.	5.05	5.	6.5
	× 6		× 7		× 3		× 8		× 13

6.	1.906	7.	7.0216	8.	6.65	9.	5.364	10.	27.035
	× 28		× 52		× 77		× 93		× 93

Complete each analogy.

EXAMPLE:

Tree is to *lumber* as *wheat* is to _____**flour**_____ .

11. *Bricks* are to *wall* as *fingers* are to _____ .

12. *Pages* are to *book* as _____ are to *the United States.*

13. *Finger* is to *hand* as *toe* is to _____ .

14. *Brake* is to *stop* as *gas pedal* is to _____ .

15. *Apple* is to *tree* as *grape* is to _____ .

16. *Foal* is to *horse* as *puppy* is to _____ .

17. *Space* is to *rocket* as _____ is to *car.*

18. *Bird* is to *nest* as *lion* is to _____ .

19. *Playwright* is to *play* as *sculptor* is to _____ .

FACTOID: Two stars that orbit each other are called *doubles.* Half of the stars in the universe are doubles.

DAY 9

To find the volume of a rectangular solid, multiply the length, width, and height of the solid. Find the volume of each figure.

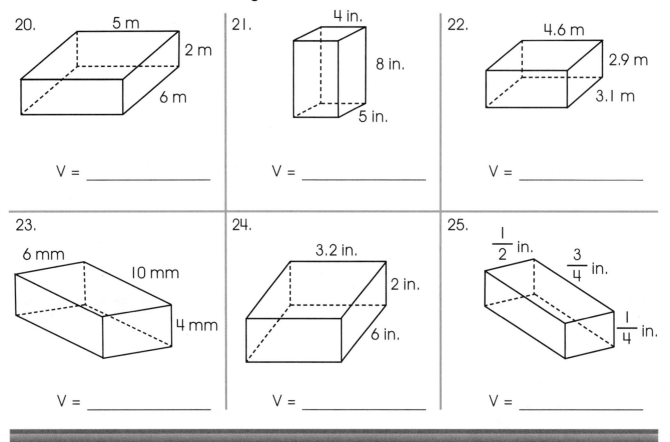

20. 5 m, 2 m, 6 m

V = _____

21. 4 in., 8 in., 5 in.

V = _____

22. 4.6 m, 2.9 m, 3.1 m

V = _____

23. 6 mm, 10 mm, 4 mm

V = _____

24. 3.2 in., 2 in., 6 in.

V = _____

25. $\frac{1}{2}$ in., $\frac{3}{4}$ in., $\frac{1}{4}$ in.

V = _____

Integrity Interviews

Having *integrity* means showing moral principles, such as honesty. Talk with several family members and neighbors. Ask them to tell you about someone they know who has integrity. Encourage the people with whom you talk to provide examples of how they see the person demonstrating integrity in her life. After completing the interviews, write a 60-second commercial promoting integrity as a way of living. Be sure to include a catchy slogan as well as a jingle. After your commercial is complete, record it and share it with family, friends, and neighbors.

FITNESS FLASH: Do 10 sit-ups.

* See page ii.

Find each quotient.

1. $3\overline{)5.4}$

2. $4\overline{)10.4}$

3. $7\overline{)25.9}$

4. $6\overline{)27.6}$

5. $0.2\overline{)17.8}$

6. $3.4\overline{)80.24}$

7. $2.5\overline{)114.75}$

8. $1.9\overline{)149.15}$

9. $3.8\overline{)262.58}$

10. $6.1\overline{)338.55}$

The noun that a pronoun refers to is called the pronoun's *antecedent*. A pronoun must agree with its antecedent. Underline the pronoun that best completes each sentence.

11. Micah and Azim stopped at the art room to pick up (their, his) paintings.

12. When Bella and Cameron arrived at the campground, (they, we) unloaded the car.

13. On Thursday, my mom and stepdad are going to the botanical gardens where (they, you) will see a new display of garden sculptures.

14. The coaches discussed (his, their) players in the teachers' lounge.

15. I asked the cashier at the grocery store, and (they, she) was very helpful.

16. Nicole and I planned (their, our) performance for weeks.

17. They like to visit parks where (they, you) can bring a dog.

18. When a person is kind to others, (he or she, you) is treated the same way in return.

CHARACTER CHECK: Share with an adult five things for which you are grateful.

DAY 10

Data can be described by how the values relate to each other and how they are spread out. Describe each set of data.

EXAMPLE: 4, 8, 9, 12, 12, 13, 14, 24, 27

Lowest value: __4__   Highest value: __27__

Spread: __23__   Center value: __12__

19. 44, 44, 45, 47, 48, 48, 49, 50, 52

Lowest value: _____   Highest value: _____

Spread: _____   Center value: _____

20. 10, 10, 25, 30, 45, 55, 80, 85, 95, 100, 100

Lowest value: _____   Highest value: _____

Spread: _____   Center value: _____

Write words from the word bank to complete the paragraph.

| Seismologists | fault | earthquake | above | epicenter |
| Seismic waves | focus | energy | beneath | fracture |

An _____ is the sudden shaking of the ground that

happens when _____ stored in rock is released. A

_____ is a break, or _____,

in the earth's crust. As rock breaks, stored energy moves along the fault. The

hypocenter, or _____, is where an earthquake begins.

The point on the earth's crust that is directly _____ the

focus is called the _____ . An earthquake begins

_____ the earth's surface. _____, or

shock waves, move out from the focus and cause the ground to shake.

_____ study and record these shock waves and determine

the size of the earthquake.

Solve each problem.

1.
```
   24.98
   14.20
   10.19
 + 82.29
```

2.
```
   89.82
   42.47
    8.18
 + 75.03
```

3.
```
  86,945
   6,913
   7,428
 + 5,317
```

4.
```
   3,921
   1,823
   4,765
 + 5,283
```

5.
```
    674
  × 392
```

6.
```
  5,978
 ×  703
```

7. $72\overline{)95,634}$

8. $82\overline{)809,791}$

9. $6\dfrac{3}{5} \times 1\dfrac{2}{8} =$ _____

10. $2\dfrac{1}{2} \times 4\dfrac{1}{5} =$ _____

11. $2\dfrac{2}{5} + 6\dfrac{3}{4} =$ _____

12. $8 - 2\dfrac{3}{4} =$ _____

A sentence should clearly indicate the noun for which a pronoun stands. Revise the underlined words to make the meaning of each sentence clear.

EXAMPLE:

When the tree hit the telephone pole, <u>it burst into flames</u>.

When the tree hit the telephone pole, the tree burst into flames.

13. When the president said good-bye to the senator, <u>he looked confident</u>.

_____

14. Marty told Ben that his scrape would heal if <u>he put antiseptic on it</u>.

_____

15. Before the key could fit the keyhole, <u>it had to be made smaller</u>.

_____

16. Graham told his dad that <u>his shirt</u> had a stain on it.

_____

Read the passage. Then, answer the questions.

from *The Story of Doctor Dolittle* by Hugh Lofting

He was very fond of animals and kept many kinds of pets. Besides the goldfish in the pond at the bottom of his garden, he had rabbits in the pantry, white mice in his piano, a squirrel in the linen closet and a hedgehog in the cellar. He had a cow with a calf too, and an old lame horse twenty-five years of age—and chickens, and pigeons, and two lambs, and many other animals. But his favorite pets were Dab-Dab the duck, Jip the dog, Gub-Gub the baby pig, Polynesia the parrot, and the owl Too-Too.

His sister used to grumble about all these animals and said they made the house untidy. And one day when an old lady with rheumatism came to see the Doctor, she sat on the hedgehog who was sleeping on the sofa and never came to see him any more, but drove every Saturday all the way to Oxenthorpe, another town ten miles off, to see a different doctor.

Then his sister, Sarah Dolittle, came to him and said, "John, how can you expect sick people to come and see you when you keep all these animals in the house? It's a fine doctor would have his parlor full of hedgehogs and mice!"

17. Based on the passage, what type of book do you think *The Story of Doctor Dolittle* is? Explain. _____

_____

_____

18. From what point of view is the story told? How might it be different if it were told from Dr. Dolittle's point of view? _____

_____

19. *The Story of Doctor Dolittle* is available as a movie and as an audiobook. Check to see if your library owns either one. Watch or listen to the story. Compare your experience reading the story and watching or listening to it.

_____

_____

_____

_____

_____

_____

DAY 12

Complete each fact family.

EXAMPLE:

78 × 42 = **3,276**

42 × 78 = **3,276**

3,276 ÷ 42 = **78**

3,276 ÷ 78 = **42**

1. 39 × 56 = 2,184

2. 95 × 37 = 3,515

3. 49 × 76 = 3,724

4. 151 × 27 = 4,077

5. 3,762 ÷ 38 = 99

6. 26,320 ÷ 47 = 560

7. 48,306 ÷ 83 = 582

8. 194 × 92 = 17,848

A *simile* is a figure of speech in which two unlike things are compared using *like* or *as*. Write the actual meaning of each simile.

9. Her voice lilted like soft music. _____

10. The cat's fur is as smooth as silk. _____

11. The water is like a sparkling sapphire. _____

12. Kristen soaked up the information like a sponge. _____

13. He stood as straight as an arrow. _____

14. Write your own simile or metaphor. _____

FITNESS FLASH: Do 10 squats.

* See page ii.

73

DAY 12

Write the missing part of each equation.

15. $67 \times \underline{\hspace{1.5cm}} = 603$

16. $\underline{\hspace{1.5cm}} \times 77 = 385$

17. $2,210 \div \underline{\hspace{1.5cm}} = 85$

18. $5,518 \div \underline{\hspace{1.5cm}} = 62$

19. $19,347 - \underline{\hspace{1.5cm}} = 18,470$

20. $23,432 + \underline{\hspace{1.5cm}} = 24,089$

21. $32 \times \underline{\hspace{1.5cm}} = 6,400$

22. $56,993 - \underline{\hspace{1.5cm}} = 55,598$

23. $\underline{\hspace{1.5cm}} + 34,561 = 40,090$

24. $50,000 \div \underline{\hspace{1.5cm}} = 1,250$

25. $19,263 + \underline{\hspace{1.5cm}} = 66,390$

26. $\underline{\hspace{1.5cm}} - 80,399 = 110,099$

You have been given the task of adding one month to the year. What would you call your month? When in the year would it occur? What would people celebrate during the month? Write a paragraph describing your new month.

_____

_____

_____

_____

_____

_____

_____

_____

_____

_____

_____

FITNESS FLASH: Do 10 lunges.

* See page ii.

A *multiple* is a number that may be divided by another number without leaving a remainder. List five multiples for each of the following numbers.

EXAMPLE:

2 ____**4, 6, 8, 10, and 12**____

1. 5 _____

2. 9 _____

3. 10 _____

4. 12 _____

Common multiples are multiples that two or more numbers share. List three common multiples for each pair of numbers.

EXAMPLE:

4 and 5 ____**20, 40, and 60**____

5. 3 and 4 _____

6. 5 and 10 _____

7. 4 and 7 _____

8. 6 and 8 _____

The *least common multiple* is the smallest multiple that two numbers share. Name the least common multiple for each pair of numbers.

EXAMPLE:

3 and 9 ____**9**____

9. 2 and 9 _____

10. 3 and 4 _____

11. 5 and 6 _____

12. 8 and 10 _____

Underline each complete subject once and circle each simple subject. Underline each complete predicate twice and draw a line through each simple predicate.

13. Carmen walks carefully along the rocky shore.

14. Pools of water collect in rocky crevices near the shore.

15. Tide pools are home to sea plants and animals.

16. Seaweed is the most common tide pool plant.

17. They provide food and shelter for a variety of animals.

18. Carmen sees spiny sea urchins attached to a rock.

19. Their mouths are on their undersides.

20. Their sharp teeth cut seaweed into little pieces.

DAY 13

A *metaphor* is a comparison of two different things without using *like* or *as*. A metaphor is an example of figurative language, or language that paints a picture in the reader's mind. Write your own metaphors.

EXAMPLE:

People are _____ mirrors; you can see yourself in them _____.

21. Sleep is _____.

22. Happiness is _____.

23. Life is _____.

24. Friendship is _____.

25. Anger is _____.

Circle the value that makes each equation or inequality true.

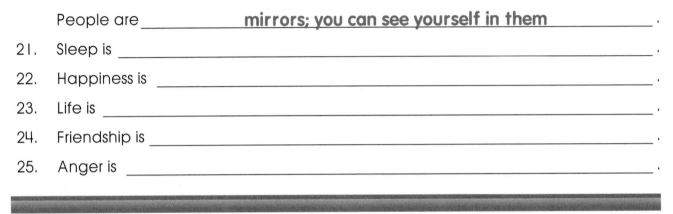

26.	27.	28.
$x + 12 = 18$	$3 \times a = 51$	$6 > 3 \times y$
4, 5, 6	15, 17, 21	1, 2, 3

29.	30.	31.
$29 < 54 - d$	$6 + m = 41$	$p - 15 = 19$
20, 25, 28	25, 35, 45	32, 34, 36

32.	33.	34.
$8 \times t = 32$	$n + 8 > 41$	$840 - s = 766$
4, 6, 8	23, 28, 38	64, 74, 78

Rewrite each expression using an exponent. Then, evaluate each expression.

EXAMPLE: $3 \times 3 \times 3 = 3^3 = 27$

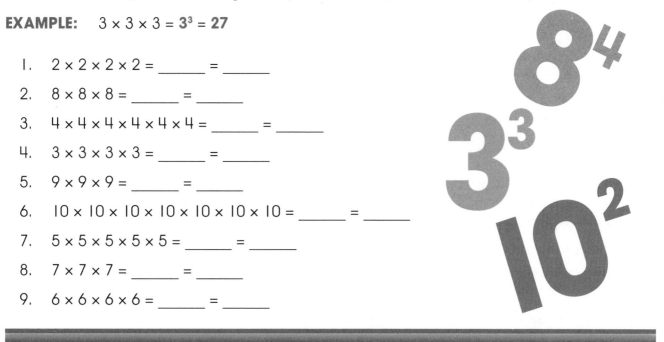

1. $2 \times 2 \times 2 \times 2 =$ _____ = _____

2. $8 \times 8 \times 8 =$ _____ = _____

3. $4 \times 4 \times 4 \times 4 \times 4 \times 4 =$ _____ = _____

4. $3 \times 3 \times 3 \times 3 =$ _____ = _____

5. $9 \times 9 \times 9 =$ _____ = _____

6. $10 \times 10 \times 10 \times 10 \times 10 \times 10 \times 10 =$ _____ = _____

7. $5 \times 5 \times 5 \times 5 \times 5 =$ _____ = _____

8. $7 \times 7 \times 7 =$ _____ = _____

9. $6 \times 6 \times 6 \times 6 =$ _____ = _____

If the sentence has a compound subject, write *CS* and circle the two simple subjects. If the sentence has a compound predicate, write *CP* and circle the two simple predicates. Write *N* if the sentence has neither a compound subject nor a compound predicate.

10.   _____   People have planted crops and raised animals for about 10,000 years.

11.   _____   The ancient Chinese and Japanese practiced freshwater and saltwater farming.

12.   _____   The Japanese raised oysters as early as 2000 BC.

13.   _____   Fish and shellfish have long been sources of protein for Southeast Asian people.

14.   _____   Overfishing and pollution led to the decline of ocean animals over the years.

15.   _____   Sea farming and ranching help restore the food supply.

16.   _____   Mariculturists, or sea farmers, raise and sell lobsters and shrimp.

17.   _____   Oysters grown on farms often grow larger and taste better than wild oysters.

Read the passage. Then, answer the questions.

The Trail of Tears

People of different cultures lived in North America before European explorers arrived. As Europeans began to settle in the New World, they competed with American Indians for land and other resources, such as gold. Over time, the New World was divided into states, and a government was formed. The U.S. government passed laws in the 1830s making it legal to force American Indians to relocate if settlers wanted their land. The Cherokee and other American Indian groups had to move from the southeastern United States to lands farther west. Thousands of American Indians traveled more than 1,000 miles (1,600 kilometers) on foot from their homelands to the land that later became the U.S. state of Oklahoma. Many people died from disease or hunger along the route. The name *Trail of Tears* was given to this event in U.S. history because of the struggles people faced on their journeys. Today, the descendants of the survivors of the Trail of Tears make up the Cherokee Nation.

18.   What is the main idea of this passage?
   A.   Many people from Europe settled in the New World.
   B.   Some American Indians still live in Oklahoma.
   C.   The Trail of Tears was the forced relocation of American Indians in the United States.

19.   What did European settlers compete with American Indians for? _____

_____

20.   How did the U.S. laws that were passed in the 1830s affect American Indians?

_____

_____

21.   Where were American Indians forced to move? _____

_____

22.   What is the Trail of Tears? _____

_____

23.   Find another account of the Trail of Tears at the library or online. An account written from a first-person point of view, as in a diary, may be especially interesting. How does the account you found differ from the passage above? On a separate sheet of paper, write a paragraph describing the similarities and differences.

Complete each sentence with an intensive pronoun from the word bank.

| himself | yourselves | herself | myself | yourself | ourselves |

1. Mischa isn't home this afternoon, so Nicole will mow the lawn _____ .

2. We were very proud of _____ when the coach handed us the first-place trophy.

3. It is time you took responsibility _____ for your belongings.

4. The judge _____ had tears in his eyes as the jury shared the decision.

5. We want all of you to ask _____ a very important question.

6. I explained the situation to the principal _____ .

A *restrictive clause* often begins with *that* or *who*. It is needed to make the meaning of the sentence clear. A *nonrestrictive clause* often begins with *which*. It can be left out and the sentence will still be clear. Nonrestrictive clauses are set off from the rest of the sentence by commas. Read each sentence. If it has a nonrestrictive clause, add commas around it. If it does not, make a check mark on the line.

EXAMPLE:

_____✓_____   The backpack that I like is on sale.

_____   *Wonderama,* which came out last summer, is Ana's favorite movie.

7. _____   My great-aunt who is an artist lives in New Mexico.

8. _____   The drawing that was done in charcoal won first prize.

9. _____   Shonda's book club which meets on the first Tuesday of each month is reading *Oliver Twist.*

10. _____   The old piano which was badly in need of tuning sat in the corner.

11. _____   The maple tree that has the bright yellow leaves was just a sapling when we moved in.

12. _____   My grandmother attended Hawthorne Elementary which was built in 1928.

DAY 15

Circle the two words that are being compared in each sentence. Then, write **S** if the comparison is a simile. Write **M** if it is a metaphor.

13. _____ The trees are like soldiers standing at attention.

14. _____ When I looked down from the airplane, the cars on the highway were as small as ants.

15. _____ The sound of waves lapping on the shore reminded me of dogs taking a long drink.

16. _____ Twenty circus clowns were like sardines packed in one car.

17. _____ The fans' stomping feet in the bleachers were beating drums.

Most earthquakes occur at plate boundaries. An *epicenter* is the place on Earth's surface above an earthquake's focus. Study the map of epicenters and answer the questions.

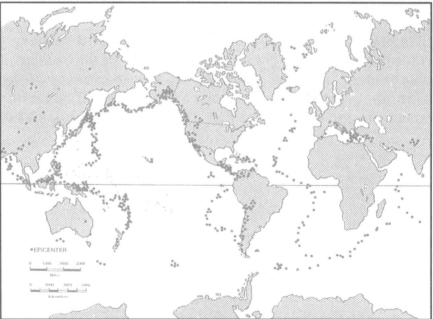

18. Draw a line around the areas with the most earthquake activity.

19. Why do most earthquakes occur at plate boundaries? _____

_____

CHARACTER CHECK: What does it mean to be optimistic?

Write the next number in each number pattern.

1. 4, 8, 16, 32, 64, _____

2. 1, 4, 7, 6, 9, 12, 11, _____

3. 1, 4, 7, 10, 13, 16, _____

4. 3, 3, 6, 5, 5, 10, 8, 8, 16, 13, 13, _____

5. 3, 5, 8, 12, 17, 23, _____

6. 6, 11, 16, 21, _____

7. 6, 36, 66, 96, _____

8. 1, 5, 9, 8, 12, 16, 15, 19, 23, 22, _____

Find the area of each figure.

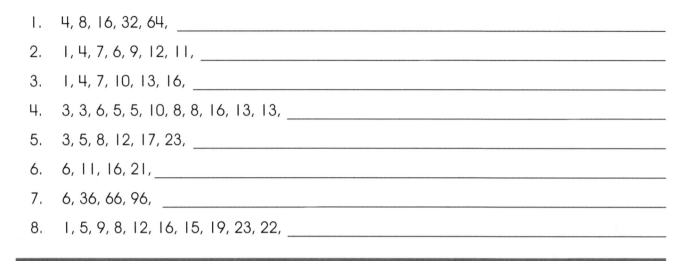

Area of a quadrilateral = length × width

Area of a triangle = $\frac{1}{2}$ × base × height

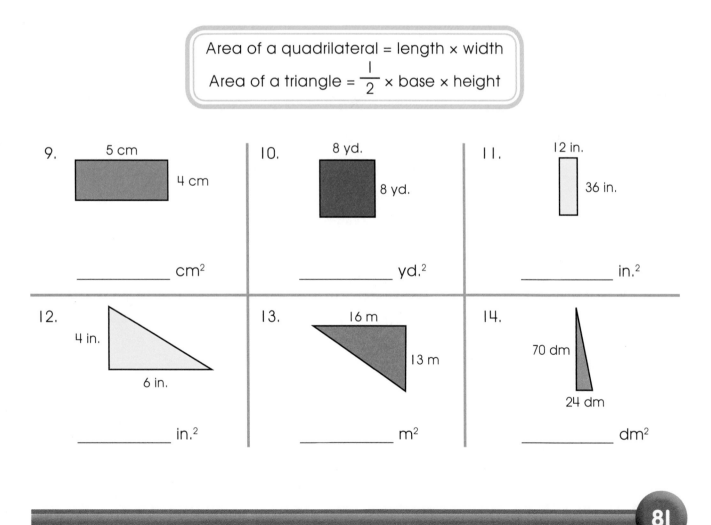

9. 5 cm, 4 cm _____ cm²

10. 8 yd., 8 yd. _____ yd.²

11. 12 in., 36 in. _____ in.²

12. 4 in., 6 in. _____ in.²

13. 16 m, 13 m _____ m²

14. 70 dm, 24 dm _____ dm²

DAY 16

Write the missing numbers in each list. Then, write the rule.

15.
M	N
15	20
40	45
90	___
35	___

Rule: **M + 5 = N**

16.
M	N
25	36
19	30
57	___
___	84

Rule: **M + 11 = N**

17.
M	N
54	45
89	80
73	___
___	61

Rule: **M –** _____

18.
M	N
48	37
12	1
___	19
24	___

Rule: _____

19.
M	N
8	48
4	24
10	___
6	___

Rule: _____

20.
M	N
21	7
30	10
18	___
12	___

Rule: _____

21.
M	N
7	63
___	81
___	54
3	27

Rule: _____

22.
M	N
10	120
___	144
9	108
___	132

Rule: _____

Read this part of the U.S. Declaration of Independence. Then, answer the questions.

We hold these truths to be self-evident, that all men are created equal, that they are endowed by their Creator with certain unalienable Rights, that among these are Life, Liberty, and the pursuit of Happiness. —That to secure these rights, Governments are instituted among Men, deriving their just powers from the consent of the governed, —That whenever any Form of Government becomes destructive of these ends, it is the Right of the People to alter or to abolish it, and to institute new Government, laying its foundation on such principles and organizing its powers in such form, as to them shall seem most likely to effect their Safety and Happiness.

23. What are the basic rights of all people according to the Declaration of Independence? _____

24. Why are governments "instituted," or created? _____

25. What should people do if they feel the government is not acting in their best interest? _____

A *factor* is a divisor of a number. A *common factor* is a divisor that is shared by two or more numbers. The *greatest common factor* is the largest common factor shared by two numbers. List the factors for each pair of numbers. Then, circle the greatest common factors.

EXAMPLE: 12: 1, 2, ③ 4, 6, 12
            15: 1, ③ 5, 15
            (The largest factor shared by both numbers is 3, so the greatest common
             factor of 12 and 15 is 3.)

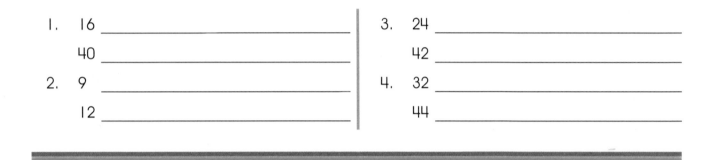

1.   16 _____

     40 _____

2.   9 _____

     12 _____

3.   24 _____

     42 _____

4.   32 _____

     44 _____

Underline the complete verb and circle the helping verb in each sentence.

EXAMPLE: Jack (was) working in town.

5.   Jasmine is walking to the park with her friends.

6.   My mother has shopped at that department store for many years.

7.   I might have called if I had known you were home.

8.   The airport is closed because of yesterday's snowstorm.

9.   Jim does enjoy sports.

10.   Mark is playing outdoors with Sam.

11.   Dana does finish her homework every day.

12.   Misty and Courtney are watching TV.

FACTOID: The Arctic permafrost can be more than 1,400 feet (426.7 m) deep.

DAY 17

Read the passage. Then, answer the questions.

The United Nations

The United Nations (UN) is a group of countries that work to promote world peace and good relationships between countries. The UN was formed in 1945, after World War II ended. People from 50 countries went to San Francisco, California, to discuss ways to encourage international cooperation. The UN's Security Council has 15 countries, of which five are permanent members (China, France, the Russian Federation, the United Kingdom, and the United States). These five countries can block proposals brought to the council by voting against them. The other countries on the council are elected to two-year terms. The UN is led by a secretary-general who serves a five-year term. The UN provides peacekeepers to countries at war, helps victims of natural disasters such as flooding, promotes workers' rights, and provides food, medicine, and safe drinking water to those in need. The organization tries to help all people, regardless of where they live.

13. What is the main idea of this passage?
    A. The United Nations helps victims of natural disasters.
    B. The United Nations works to promote peace around the world.
    C. The United Nations was formed in 1945.

14. After what world event was the United Nations formed?_____

    _____

15. What can the five permanent members of the Security Council do?

    _____

16. How long does the secretary-general serve?_____

17. What are three ways that the United Nations helps people around the world?

    _____

    _____

    _____

FITNESS FLASH: Do five push-ups.

Express each as a ratio in simplest form.

EXAMPLE: There are 2 cans of corn and 5 cans of beans in the cupboard. Write the ratio of cans of corn to cans of beans in the cupboard. $\frac{2}{5}$

1. There are 4 green marbles and 8 red marbles in a bag. Write the ratio of green marbles to red marbles.

   _____

2. There are 12 cars and 3 motorcycles in a parking lot. Write the ratio of cars to motorcycles.

   _____

3. There are 10 soccer balls and 15 footballs in a storeroom. Write the ratio of soccer balls to footballs.

   _____

4. There are 11 dogs and 4 cats at a kennel. Write the ratio of dogs to cats.

   _____

5. There are 8 quarters and 3 dimes in a coin purse. Write the ratio of quarters to dimes.

   _____

6. There are 12 robins and 15 chickadees in a tree. Write the ratio of robins to chickadees.

   _____

Combine each pair of sentences to write a compound sentence using *and* or *but*. In each new sentence, place a comma before the conjunction.

7. The frogs sleep during the day. They hunt for food at night.

   _____

   _____

8. A parrot's bright colors are easy to see in a tree. A tree boa's green color makes it difficult to spot.

   _____

   _____

9. A fruit bat has a long nose. It has large eyes to help it see in the dark.

   _____

   _____

DAY 18

An *idiom* is a phrase that states one thing but means another. Draw a line to match each idiom with its meaning.

EXAMPLE: It was raining cats and dogs. ———————— It was raining hard.

10. I can do math problems standing on my head.

Who told the secret?

11. Who let the cat out of the bag?

She will sleep very well tonight.

12. Charlie is a chip off the old block.

I know math well.

13. Jenna will sleep like a log.

The two friends are very similar.

14. Cora and Alexis are like two peas in a pod.

He is just like his father.

Write *T* for true or *F* for false for each statement.

15. _____ A volcano is an opening in the crust of the earth through which lava, gases, ash, and rocks erupt.

16. _____ Volcanic material can build up to form mountains.

17. _____ These mountains can form only on land.

18. _____ All magma comes from Earth's core.

19. _____ Most volcanoes happen underwater.

20. _____ Mid-ocean ridges form when magma rises to fill a gap between diverging tectonic plates.

21. _____ Most volcanoes on land occur at diverging plate boundaries.

22. _____ Volcanoes on land occur on the edges of continents or on islands.

23. _____ When two plates converge, compression forces rocks upward to make mountains.

FACTOID: Iceland is a nation built on volcanoes.

The *distributive property* states: $a \times (b + c) = (a \times b) + (a \times c)$. The same property also means that: $a \times (b - c) = (a \times b) - (a \times c)$. The distributive property can help simplify complex math problems. Rewrite each expression using the distributive property. Then, solve.

EXAMPLE:

$21 \times 13 =$ ___ $(21 \times 10) + (21 \times 3) = 210 + 63$ ___ $=$ ___ 273 ___

1. $12 \times 55 =$ _____ $=$ ___
2. $61 \times 15 =$ _____ $=$ ___
3. $45 \times 22 =$ _____ $=$ ___
4. $16 \times 47 =$ _____ $=$ ___
5. $37 \times 102 =$ _____ $=$ ___
6. $64 \times 13 =$ _____ $=$ ___
7. $48 \times 44 =$ _____ $=$ ___
8. $33 \times 32 =$ _____ $=$ ___

Armloads of Strength!

Collect empty water or soft drink bottles of different sizes and fill each bottle halfway with water, sand, or pebbles. Use your bottles for arm curls to improve your strength.

Hold a bottle by your side. Standing with your feet shoulder-width apart, turn your hand so that your palm is faceup. Pull your hand slowly toward your chest and inhale deeply. As you exhale, lower your hand by your side. Do 8–10 repetitions and switch arms. As you become stronger, fill your bottle with increasing amounts of water, sand, or pebbles. With a marker, draw a line for each increment to track your progress.

FACTOID: Walruses can walk on all four fins as fast as a person can run.

DAY 19

Choose the correct meaning of the bold idiom in each sentence.

9. He is a **big cheese** at his school.
   A. cafeteria worker
   B. principal
   C. very important person

10. My dad is the **top dog** at his job.
    A. loudest one
    B. parts supplier
    C. one in charge; boss

11. After working all afternoon in the yard, Dad and I decided to **call it a day** and go to dinner.
    A. stop
    B. talk
    C. rake leaves

12. She did not talk about her family because she did not want to reveal the **skeletons in her closet**.
    A. her family secrets
    B. where she kept trash
    C. the end of a scary story

13. Tommy would **give you the shirt off his back** if necessary.
    A. lend you a shirt
    B. help any way he could
    C. keep you warm

14. Maria had the answer to Connor's question **on the tip of her tongue**.
    A. unable to think of the answer
    B. could not talk
    C. remembered

If you could live in one time period in history, which period would you choose? Why? What do you think your life would be like on a daily basis? (What would you wear? What would you eat? What would you do for fun?) Write a paragraph about your life in that time period.

_____

_____

_____

_____

_____

_____

FITNESS FLASH: Do 10 sit-ups.

* See page ii.

Translate each description into an algebraic expression. Then, evaluate the expression using the value shown in the box for the variable.

$a = 3$	$b = 2$	$c = 5$	$d = 7$
$w = 1$	$x = 12$	$y = 9$	$z = 4$

EXAMPLE:

the product of 3 and a added to 12 = __(3 x a) + 12__ = __21__ when ____$a = 3$____

1. y times 12 = _____ = ___ when _____

2. the quotient of 36 and b = _____ = ___ when _____

3. 14 added to w = _____ = ___ when _____

4. the product of z and 6 divided by 12 = _____ = ___ when _____

5. c to the second power times 2 = _____ = ___ when _____

6. the difference of d and 15 divided by 4 = _____ = ___ when _____

7. 23 added to the quotient of x and 6 = _____ = ___ when _____

Fill in the spaces in the table below.

Word	Latin or Greek Root	Root's Meaning
thermostat	_____	_____
_____	bi	two
meteorology	_____	_____
_____	rupt	_____
monarchy	_____	_____
pedestrian	_____	foot
_____	audi	_____
reject	_____	throw

Read the passage. Then, answer the questions.

Meteorologists

Most people have seen weather forecasters on TV. People who study the weather are called *meteorologists*. Most of their jobs are performed off camera in offices or laboratories where they study the weather. Meteorologists study past weather patterns to help them predict future weather. They take readings of temperature, wind speed, atmospheric pressure, and precipitation (rain or snow) to forecast the weather. They may use satellites, airplanes, and weather balloons to collect additional data. Meteorologists develop computer models to predict how climate and weather might change in the future. They also study how weather phenomena, such as tornadoes, form. An important part of a meteorologist's job is giving people accurate information in case of an emergency. If your community is being threatened by a storm, such as a hurricane, you need to know when it might strike and how to stay safe.

8. What is the main idea of this passage?

   A.   Weather forecasters often appear on TV.

   B.   Tornadoes and hurricanes can cause great damage.

   C.   Meteorologists study the weather.

9. Why do meteorologists study weather patterns of the past? _____

   _____

10. What does a meteorologist consider when forecasting the weather? _____

   _____

   _____

11. How can computer models help? _____

   _____

12. What might a meteorologist tell you about a hurricane? _____

   _____

13. Watch a local weather forecast on TV. How does the meteorologist's presentation compare to the information about meteorologists you read in the passage above?

   _____

   _____

   _____

Paper Airplane

The paper airplane you will create in this activity demonstrates the movement of an airplane in response to the air through which it is traveling. If you work on your design carefully, you can get your airplane to soar like an eagle!

Materials
• sheet of paper (8 ½" x 11")
• scissors
• tape

Procedure

1. Fold the upper edge of the paper to the opposite side of the paper. (A) Unfold and repeat with the other side. You should now have an X on your page. Fold the top to the bottom of the X created by the first two folds. (B)

2. Fold in the middle crease on both sides, bringing the top corners toward the bottom of the X. Now, the paper should look like a house. (C)

3. Fold the tip of the roof to the gutter. (D)

4. Fold the airplane in half so that the folds are not showing. (E)

5. Fold down the wings. The body of the airplane should be no more than a half inch (1.27 cm) tall. (F)

6. Fold the outer quarter inch (0.635 cm) of the airplane wing. Tape the two wings together at the middle fold. (G)

7. Cut two small flaps in the back of the wings in the sections illustrated. These will help direct the movement of the airplane. (G)

8. By bending the flaps on the back of the wing, you can get the airplane to bank either left or right. If you bend both flaps the same way, you can get the airplane to climb sharply into the atmosphere.

A.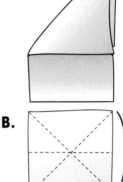

B.

C.

D.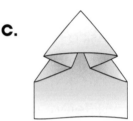

E.

F.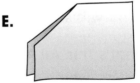

G.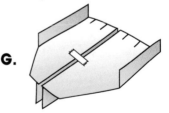

BONUS

Human Nerves

People are able to feel because we have nerves. Some places in our bodies have more nerves than others. Complete this activity to see which places have more nerves and are more sensitive.

Materials
• partner
• paper clip

Procedure
1. Open the paper clip so that the two endpoints are pointing in the same direction, at least one inch (2.54 cm) apart.
2. Ask a partner to place his arm on a table and to close his eyes. You will touch the paper clip's endpoints to different parts of his fingers and arm to see if he can tell whether you are using one end of the paper clip or two.
3. Begin by touching his fingertips with two endpoints. Ask him if he feels one or two points. Tell him whether he is correct or incorrect. Repeat with several different fingers, changing from one to two points and back again.
4. Slowly test your partner's nerves by touching the points to his mid-fingers, palms, wrists, and both sides of the forearm. Change from one to two points at random.

What's This All About?
Nerves, which detect when a body part is touched, are distributed all over the human body. However, nerves are not distributed evenly. By finding out where your partner can feel both ends of the paper clip, you also find out where the body's nerves are closest together. What do you notice about the function of the body parts that seem to have a lot of nerves?

The Mayflower Compact

Read the passage. Then, circle *fact* or *opinion* for each statement.

The Pilgrims were a group of people who disagreed with how the Church of England was run. They wanted to go to a place where they could establish their own church. They received permission to travel to Virginia, where they could worship as they pleased. In September of 1620, about 50 Pilgrims and about 50 other Englishmen (whom the Pilgrims called "Strangers") set sail for America on a ship called the *Mayflower*. In November of 1620, the ship arrived at Cape Cod in present-day Massachusetts. The water to the south was too rough and dangerous, so they decided to settle where they were.

Because the trip had not turned out as planned, some of the Strangers talked about leaving the group. However, the group believed that they had a better chance for survival if they all stuck together, and they had a better chance of sticking together if they agreed at the start to follow certain rules. They wrote an agreement called the *Mayflower Compact*. Many people consider the Mayflower Compact to be the first form of self-government in America's history. The document declared that the group would stay together and form their own laws and government. All who signed promised to follow these laws. Forty-one men signed the compact. (Women did not sign because the did not have many rights at that time.) They elected John Carver as their first governor and set out to look for fresh water. After exploring the area, the travelers decided to settle nearby in Plymouth.

1. The Pilgrims' ideas about the church were better than England's ideas.   fact   opinion

2. The *Mayflower* sailed in 1620.   fact   opinion

3. Signing the Mayflower Compact was a good idea.   fact   opinion

4. Forty-one men signed the Mayflower Compact.   fact   opinion

5. John Carver was the smartest person on the *Mayflower*.   fact   opinion

6. About 100 people traveled to America on the *Mayflower*.   fact   opinion

7. The *Mayflower* did not land where the Pilgrims had planned.   fact   opinion

8. The Mayflower Compact was a perfect agreement.   fact   opinion

BONUS

The Branches of the U.S. Government

Write the name of the U.S. branch of government (legislative, executive, or judicial) for each responsibility.

1. can impeach the president   _____

2. writes bills   _____

3. approves or vetoes bills   _____

4. interprets and examines laws   _____

5. appoints justices   _____

The U.S. government is divided into three branches. Each branch is given different but equal powers. Write the responsibilities of each branch in the pie chart.

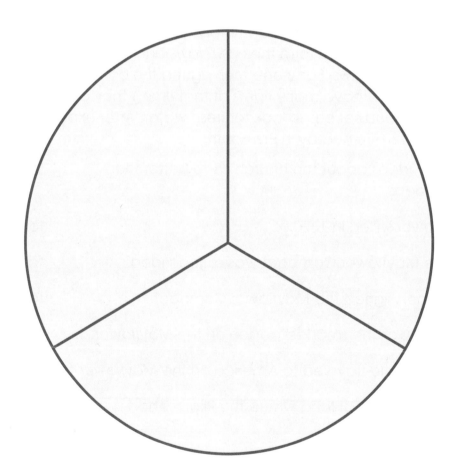

Reading Rainfall Maps

Precipitation maps, or rainfall maps, use patterns to show areas with varying amounts of rainfall or snow. Compare the precipitation maps of Arizona and the main island of Hawaii.

Annual Rainfall

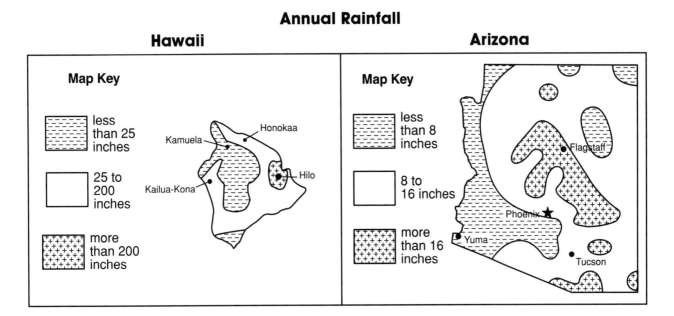

1. Which state receives more rainfall? _____

2. How much annual rainfall does Hilo, Hawaii, receive? _____

3. What does ▦ on the Arizona map represent? _____

4. What does ▦ on the Hawaii map represent? _____

5. Which city is in the driest area in Hawaii? _____

6. Which city on the Arizona map receives the most rainfall? _____

7. Which two cities in Arizona receive 8 to 16 inches (20.32 to 40.64 cm) of

   rain annually? _____ and _____

8. Which two cities in Hawaii receive 25 to 200 inches (63.5 to 508 cm) of

   rain annually? _____ and _____

BONUS

Take It Outside!

Invite family members to go with you to an outdoor market. Be sure to bring a pen and a notebook. Once at the market, begin your hunt for decimals. As you travel the aisles, look at prices. When you locate a decimal, write down the decimal's location and how it is used. On your return home, have some fun with your decimal discoveries. Make a poster informing others of the various "hiding" places decimals have at the market.

Weekends in the summer provide a wonderful opportunity for your family to get together with neighbors for some fun. Invite your family and neighbors to join you for an afternoon paper airplane competition. Provide people with paper to make their airplanes. Have a tape measure available to measure the flight distances. Ask people to take turns flying their paper airplanes. After each throw, measure the distance and list the distance on a chart. After everyone has flown her paper airplane, check the chart and announce the winner of the paper airplane neighborhood competition.

With a family member, go for a walk in a local park. Bring a pencil and a notebook. As you explore the park, keep track of what is in the park and where park attractions are located. Once you are familiar with the park, find a place to sit with your family member and make a map. Be sure to include a compass rose with direction arrows and a key for symbols used on the map. Then, share your map with friends to assist them in finding their way around the park.

Monthly Goals

Think of three goals to set for yourself this month. For example, you may want to learn five new vocabulary words each week. Write your goals on the lines. Post them someplace visible, where you will see them every day.

Draw a line through each goal as you meet it. Feel proud that you have met your goals and set new ones to continue to challenge yourself.

1. _____

2. _____

3. _____

Word List

The following words are used in this section. Use a dictionary to look up each word that you do not know. Then, write three sentences. Use a word from the word list in each sentence.

attire
gigantic
hazardous
median
ornately

prestigious
punctual
revolution
sapling
Shoshone

1. _____

_____

2. _____

_____

3. _____

_____

Introduction to Endurance

This section includes fitness and character development activities that focus on endurance. These activities are designed to get you moving and thinking about developing your physical and mental stamina.

Physical Endurance

What do climbing stairs, jogging, and riding your bike have in common? They are all great ways to build endurance!

Having endurance means performing an activity for a period of time before your body becomes tired. Improving your endurance requires regular aerobic exercise, which causes your heart to beat faster. You also breathe harder. As a result of regular aerobic activity, your heart becomes stronger and your blood cells deliver oxygen to your body more efficiently.

Summer provides numerous opportunities to improve your endurance. Although there are times when a relaxing activity is valuable, it is important to take advantage of the warm mornings and sunny days to go outside. Choose activities that you enjoy. Invite a family member to go on a walk or a bicycle ride. Play a game of basketball with friends. Leave the relaxing activities for when it is dark, too hot, or raining.

Set an endurance goal this summer. For example, you might jog every day until you can run one mile without stopping. Set new goals when you meet your old ones. Be proud of your endurance success!

Mental Endurance

Endurance applies to the mind as well as to the body. Showing mental endurance means sticking with something. You can show mental endurance every day. Staying with a task when you might want to quit and continuing until it is finished are ways that you can show mental endurance.

Build your mental endurance this summer. Maybe you want to earn some extra money for a new bike by helping your neighbors with yard work. But, after one week of working in your neighbors' yards, you discover that it is not as easy as you thought that it would be. Think about some key points, such as how you have wanted that new bike for months. Be positive. Remind yourself that you have been working for only one week and that your neighbors are very appreciative of your work. Think of ways to make the yard work more enjoyable, such as starting earlier in the day or listening to music while you work. Quitting should be the last resort.

Build your mental endurance now. It will help prepare you for challenges you may face later.

Find the area of each figure.

> The area of a parallelogram = base × height.

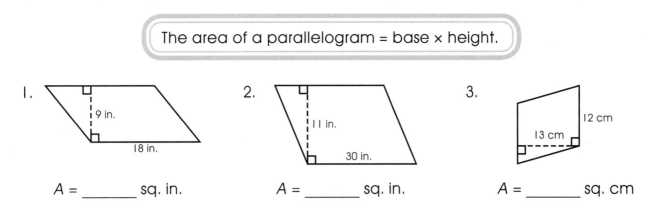

1. 9 in.
    18 in.

    A = _____ sq. in.

2. 11 in.
    30 in.

    A = _____ sq. in.

3. 12 cm
    13 cm

    A = _____ sq. cm

To find the area of an irregular shape, separate the shape into two or more smaller figures. Find the area of each part and then add them together.

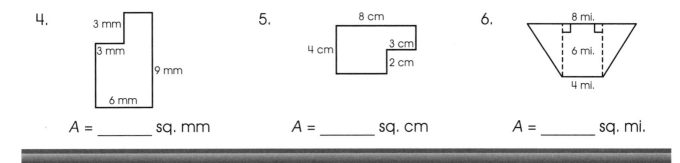

4. 3 mm
    3 mm
    9 mm
    6 mm

    A = _____ sq. mm

5. 8 cm
    4 cm   3 cm
            2 cm

    A = _____ sq. cm

6. 8 mi.
    6 mi.
    4 mi.

    A = _____ sq. mi.

Write *I* or *me* to correctly complete each sentence.

EXAMPLE: She and ____I____ baked a cake.

7. Mom and _____ went to the store.

8. Will you come to see Ken and _____?

9. Ann Marie and _____ ate our lunches outside.

10. The gift was sent by Aunt Jean and _____.

Circle the possessive pronoun that correctly completes each sentence.

11. (Her, hers) handwriting is very neat.

12. The prize is (his, our).

13. (My, Mine) uncle Clint is coming for a visit.

14. The book you loaned to Leza was (my, mine).

DAY I

A negative number is a number that has a value of less than zero. A positive number is a number that is greater than zero. Write the negative numbers on the number line.

15.

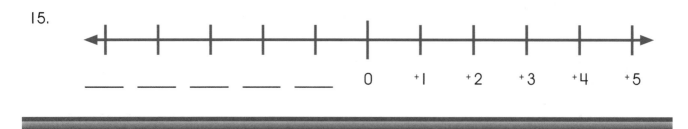

_____ _____ _____ _____ _____ 0   +1   +2   +3   +4   +5

Read the passage. Then, answer the questions.

Sacagawea

A U.S. gold dollar coin shows the image of a young American Indian woman named Sacagawea and her baby. In 1800, when Sacagawea was about 12 years old, an enemy tribe captured her. They took her far away from her Shoshone home. Four years later, Sacagawea joined a group of explorers who wanted to find a way to the Pacific Ocean. Meriwether Lewis and William Clark would lead the group across the American Northwest. Sacagawea went with her husband. Her baby son was strapped to her back. She was the only woman in the group of explorers.

Sacagawea helped make the trip a success. In May of 1805, she jumped into the river to save the explorers' journals that had fallen out of the canoe. Sacagawea found edible plants for the men and acted as interpreter when they met different tribes of American Indians. In August of 1805, the explorers came upon a group of Shoshones. The chief was Sacagawea's brother, whom she had not seen in five years. The tribe gave the explorers the food, guides, and horses they needed to finish their journey and to return home safely. Sacagawea had helped them greatly.

16. What is the main idea of the second paragraph?
    A. Sacagawea helped the explorers survive.
    B. The explorers made discoveries during exploration.
    C. Sacagawea saw the Pacific Ocean.

17. What area did Lewis and Clark plan to explore? _____

FACTOID: An elephant seal can hold its breath for up to two hours.

DAY 2

A pronoun that is part of the subject of a sentence is called a *subject pronoun.*
A pronoun that is not part of the subject is an *object pronoun.* Write *SP* if the
underlined pronoun is a subject pronoun. Write *OP* if it is an object pronoun.

1. _____ The funny story made <u>us</u> laugh.

2. _____ Did <u>they</u> fly or take the train home?

3. _____ Ted held the trophy in front of McCall and <u>her</u>.

4. _____ <u>We</u> are going to Maine this summer.

5. _____ Will <u>we</u> see any sharks at Sea Life Park?

6. _____ Are <u>you</u> a cousin of Hal Tomyn?

7. _____ Denise and <u>I</u> went ice-skating with her family.

8. _____ The dog found <u>it</u> under the kitchen table.

9. _____ Do not give <u>her</u> the present until noon.

10. _____ I bought blue gym shoes this year because I like <u>them</u>.

The *absolute value* of a number is its distance from zero on a number line. Absolute
value is shown by vertical lines on either side of an integer. Write the absolute value
of each integer.

EXAMPLE:

| 8 | ___**8**___

| –8 | ___**8**___

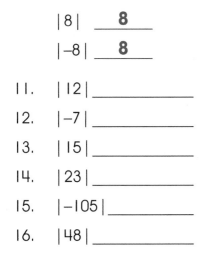

11. | 12 | _____

12. | –7 | _____

13. | 15 | _____

14. | 23 | _____

15. | –105 | _____

16. | 48 | _____

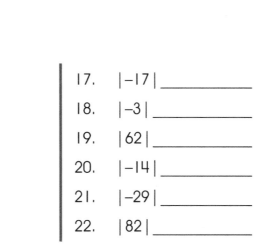

17. | –17 | _____

18. | –3 | _____

19. | 62 | _____

20. | –14 | _____

21. | –29 | _____

22. | 82 | _____

DAY 2

Look up the word *dramatize* in a dictionary. Then, answer the questions.

23. What are the guide words on the page? _____

24. How many meanings are listed for *dramatize*? _____

25. Write the word. Write the pronunciation. _____

26. How many syllables does the word have? _____

27. What does *dramatize* mean in this sentence?

    Do you always have to <u>dramatize</u>, Annie?

    _____

28. Write the other forms of the word given in the dictionary and tell what part of

    speech they are. _____

29. List two words on the same page as *dramatize*. Write their pronunciations.

    _____

Pretend that you live in the year 2028. How will life be different? How will you look? What will you eat? How will you get around? Write a detailed paragraph and draw a picture on a separate sheet of paper to describe and show what you imagine.

_____

_____

_____

_____

_____

_____

_____

 FITNESS FLASH: Jog in place for 30 seconds.

* See page ii.

In each situation, find the rate.

1. You drive 220 miles in 4 hours. What is the rate per hour?

_____

2. Your heart beats 234 times each minute. What is the rate per second?

_____

3. You pay $1.68 for 6 cans of soda. What is the rate per soda?

_____

4. It snows 3 inches in 4 hours. What is the rate per hour?

_____

5. You type 240 words in 5 minutes. What is the rate per minute?

_____

6. You spend $3.40 for a 20-ounce box of cereal. What is the rate per ounce?

_____

7. You pay $1.30 for a 5-pound bag of potatoes. What is the rate per pound?

_____

8. You consume 13,300 calories in 7 days. What is the rate per day?

_____

9. You spend $2.25 for a 0.5-gallon container of frozen yogurt. What is the rate per gallon?

_____

10. You pay $10.80 for 8 gallons of cider. What is the rate per gallon?

_____

Circle the letter in front of the correct meaning for each root word. Then, write two words that contain that root.

11. **chron**   A. time   B. fear   C. study of

_____   _____

12. **astr**   A. life   B. stars   C. earth

_____   _____

13. **path**   A. feeling   B. fear   C. small

_____   _____

14. **bio**   A. sea   B. pull   C. life

_____   _____

DAY 3

Read the passage. Then, answer the questions.

The Post Office

In the United States and Canada, the post office is where people buy stamps and mail letters and packages. Postal employees sort mail by region and send it out for delivery on foot, by car, by truck, or by airplane. A country's national post office sets the rates for mailing materials. The cost of postage depends on the size and weight of an item, the distance to its destination, and its target delivery date. Sending the items to arrive the next day costs more than sending them by general delivery, which may take days or weeks. Some post offices offer services such as processing passport applications, banking, and selling greeting cards. Canada Post, the postal service in Canada, is run by the government. The U.S. Postal Service is part of the executive branch of the government but is run independently. Both government postal organizations face competition from private postal companies that may offer faster mail delivery at a lower cost.

15. What is the main idea of this passage?
    A.   Mail is sorted by region.
    B.   The Canadian postal service is called Canada Post.
    C.   The post office is important for communicating by mail.

16. Why do people visit post offices? _____

    _____

17. How do postal employees transport mail? _____

    _____

18. Who determines the rates for mailing materials? _____

    _____

19. What does the cost of postage depend on? _____

    _____

FACTOID: Approximately 2,000 thunderstorms are happening around the world right now.

Equivalent expressions are created by simplifying values and combining terms. If the expression includes exponents, calculate the values before simplifying: $3^2 = 9$. If the expression contains repeated addition, use multiplication instead: $x + x + x = 3x$. Create equivalent expressions.

EXAMPLE: $3(12x + 5) = $ <u>**36x + 15**</u>

1. $4(y + y + y + y) = $ _____

2. $12(5y - 3) = $ _____

3. $2^3(5g + 2) = $ _____

4. $x(x + 8) = $ _____

5. $25(3 - 4n) = $ _____

6. $8(z + z + z + z) = $ _____

7. $4^2(2x + 4) - 12 = $ _____

8. $5(3y + 13) = $ _____

9. $4(2w^2 - 4) = $ _____

10. $15(3c - 2) = $ _____

11. $6(k + k + k - 7) = $ _____

12. $12 \div (a + a + a) = $ _____

Writing is more interesting when a variety of sentence structures are used. Write a sentence to fit each description.

13. Write a sentence with a simple subject and simple predicate with adjectives, articles, and adverbs.

_____

14. Write a sentence with a direct object and an indirect object.

_____

15. Write a sentence with two prepositional phrases.

_____

16. Write a sentence with a compound subject and/or verb.

_____

DAY 4

Write *yes* or *no to* answer each question. Use a dictionary if you need help.

17. Would a boy wear a *mukluk*? _____

18. Could you work as a *gofer*? _____

19. Do you wear a *goatee* on your arm? _____

20. Could you play with a *googol*? _____

21. Is a *truffle* a rich chocolate candy? _____

22. Could you plant a *vetch*? _____

23. Does *yep* mean yes? _____

24. Is a *yeti* mysterious? _____

25. Could animals be kept in a *scribe*? _____

26. Is an *orlop* deck part of a ship? _____

27. Can you live in a *yurt*? _____

28. Would you chop wood with an *italic*? _____

29. Could you eat a *mango*? _____

30. Can you drive an *osier*? _____

31. Is a *gizzard* a kind of bird? _____

Climbing to Endurance

Climbing stairs is an easy way to improve your endurance, and this activity can be done almost anywhere. Head to a gymnasium, stadium, office, or apartment building and find several flights of stairs. Begin by walking up the stairs. Be careful to place your foot firmly on each stair, hold on to the railing, and watch out for people who may be descending. For a challenge, or as your endurance improves, wear a backpack filled with several books as you climb your way to improved endurance.

FITNESS FLASH: Hop on your right foot for 30 seconds.

* See page ii.

A number line can be used to represent the possible values of a variable. In the example below, the open circle shows that the values do not include 8. For inequalities that use ≥ (greater than or equal to) or ≤ (less than or equal to), a closed circle indicates that the values do include that point. Solve each inequality. Represent the possible values of the variable using the number line.

EXAMPLE:

$x > 3 + 5$

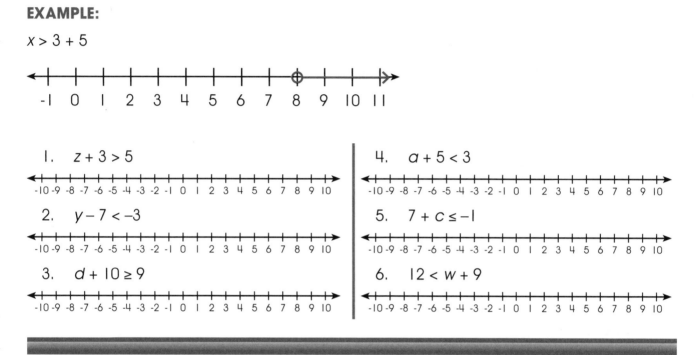

1. $z + 3 > 5$

2. $y - 7 < -3$

3. $d + 10 \geq 9$

4. $a + 5 < 3$

5. $7 + c \leq -1$

6. $12 < w + 9$

Many words have *denotations* (definitions) as well as *connotations* (feelings and values associated with the word). For example, the denotation of both *clever* and *shrewd* is "smart." However, *clever* has a more positive connotation, while *shrewd* has a more negative connotation. Match each word with another word that has a similar denotation but different connotation. Write the letter of the matching word on the line.

7. _____ thrifty

8. _____ childlike

9. _____ odor

10. _____ odd

11. _____ dog

12. _____ escape

13. _____ starving

14. _____ demand

a. scent

b. request

c. depart

d. stingy

e. hungry

f. unique

g. mutt

h. immature

DAY 5

Write an *X* beside the word or phrase that is a synonym for the first word in each list. Use a thesaurus if you need help.

15. **bronco**
_____ panther
_____ horse
_____ insect

16. **fanfare**
_____ explanation
_____ metal
_____ music

17. **residence**
_____ payment
_____ home
_____ disease

18. **narrative**
_____ complaint
_____ length
_____ story

19. **sapling**
_____ young plant
_____ vitamin
_____ young tree

20. **attire**
_____ medal
_____ wisdom
_____ clothing

- The *range* is the difference between the highest and lowest numbers in a set of data.
- To calculate the *mean* (or average), add the list of numbers and divide by the number of items.
- The *median* is the middle number that appears in the data when it is arranged in numeric order.
- The *mode* is the number that appears most often in the data.

Use the chart to answer the questions about the number of medals awarded at a recent Olympic Games.

21. What is the range of the data?

_____

22. What is the mode of the data?

_____

23. What is the median of the data?

_____

24. What is the mean number of medals awarded? _____

Country	Number of Medals
United States	91
Russia	88
China	59
Australia	58
Germany	56
Italy	34
Cuba	29
Great Britain	28
South Korea	28

CHARACTER CHECK: Talk with an adult about someone you know who shows determination.

Use equal ratios to solve each problem.

1. The Dollar-Mart grocery store sells 6 bars of soap for $1.00. How many bars of soap can a customer buy with $9.00?

2. Kelsey's soccer team scored 5 points in 2 games. At this rate, how many points will the team score in 16 games?

3. The O'Neil family is driving 60 miles per hour. If they continue to drive at this speed, how many miles will they drive in 4 hours?

Complete the table.

	Regular Price	Discount Rate	Discount	Sale Price
4.	$24	40%		
5.	$25	30%		
6.	$80	15%		
7.	$220	60%		
8.	$90	55%		
9.	$120	45%		
10.	$1,250	25%		

DAY 6

Read the passage. Then, answer the questions.

North American Pioneers

Many early North American pioneers came from Europe. Some came to pursue religious freedom, while others wanted more land for their families. Many settlers built villages along the shores of lakes, rivers, and the ocean. Water was important not only for drinking, farming, and washing clothes, but also for powering mills and traveling to other settlements. Most pioneers worked as farmers. They had to clear the land of trees before they could plant many crops. Pioneers also raised horses and oxen to help pull wagons and sheep to provide wool. When there were enough children in a village, parents sometimes built a schoolhouse and hired a teacher. Usually, all of the children were taught in a single room. Otherwise, children might be educated at home. As villages grew in size, they sometimes built a doctor's office, a blacksmith's shop, and a general store where goods were sold.

11. What is the main idea of this passage?
    A.   Some pioneers came from Europe.
    B.   Pioneer children sometimes studied at home.
    C.   Most early pioneers were farmers who lived in small villages.

12. Why did the early pioneers come to North America? _____
    _____

13. Which animals did pioneers often raise? _____
    _____

14. How were pioneer children educated? _____
    _____

15. What other buildings might a pioneer village include? _____
    _____

FACTOID: Seventy percent of Earth's surface is water.

Convert each measurement.

12 inches (in.) = 1 foot (ft.)
3 ft. = 1 yard (yd.)

1. 12 in. = _____ ft.   2. 18 in. = _____ ft.   3. 2 ft. = _____ in.

4. 48 in. = _____ ft.   5. 6 ft. = _____ yd.   6. 7 yd. = _____ ft.

7. 1 yd. = _____ in.   8. 9 ft. = _____ yd.   9. 3 yd. = _____ ft.

10. 6 in. = _____ ft.   11. 10 yd. = _____ ft.   12. 11 ft. = _____ in.

Each sentence contains informal language. Read the sentence carefully and then rewrite it on the line below using standard English.

13. "I thought the concert was totally off the hook," said Marissa.

_____

14. That construction across the street is really driving me nuts.

_____

15. Thanks a bunch for filling me in about what's going on.

_____

16. We've only got a few minutes before the bell, so you've got to get it done ASAP.

_____

17. Anyways, there was this humungous traffic jam that held things up forever.

_____

18. Their family is really loaded, so the cost of the tickets will be no big deal for them.

_____

DAY 7

Read the partial table of contents and index from a history book. Then, answer the questions.

19. What is the difference between the table of contents and the index in a book?

    _____

    _____

20. If you wanted to see if there was a picture of Andrew Jackson in the book, where would you look? _____

21. Where would you look to find out who fought in the Civil War?_____

    _____

22. How many sections are in Chapter Five?_____

23. On what page could you look to learn who Massasoit was? _____

FITNESS FLASH: Hop on your left foot 10 times.

* See page ii.

Convert each measurement.

| 1 kilometer (km) = 1,000 meters (m) | 10 dm = 100 centimeters (cm) |
| 1 m = 10 decimeters (dm) | 100 cm = 1,000 millimeters (mm) |

1. 25 cm = _____ mm

2. 3 m = _____ mm

3. 9 dm = _____ mm

4. 10 dm = _____ mm

5. 12 m = _____ mm

6. 8 m = _____ cm

7. 50 mm = _____ cm

8. 100 m = _____ cm

9. 4 km = _____ cm

Choose a work of fiction from the library, your home bookshelves, or the Summer Reading List on pages ix–x. Describe how the author develops the point of view of the narrator in the book you choose. Does the reader know everything the narrator thinks and feels? How does the narrator's point of view shape the story?

_____

_____

_____

_____

_____

_____

_____

_____

_____

_____

_____

_____

_____

DAY 8

Read the following passage. Then, answer the questions.

Timbuktu

Timbuktu is a small trading town in central Mali, located near the southern edge of the Sahara Desert. Established around AD 1100, it was a trading post for products from North and West Africa. Northern camel caravans traded salt, cloth, cowrie shells, and copper for gold, kola nuts, ivory, and slaves who came from the south.

Timbuktu's location left it open to attack, and control of the city changed many times. It has been ruled by the Mali Empire, the Songhai Empire, Morocco, nomads, France, and others. It is not as important or populated as it once was. Many of its mud and brick buildings are eroding and are half-buried in the sand.

10.   Underline the topic sentence of the passage.

11.   Circle the main idea of the first paragraph.

12.   Circle the main idea of the second paragraph.

To find the *surface area* of a rectangular prism, first find the area of each side. Then, add to find the sum. Find the surface area of each figure.

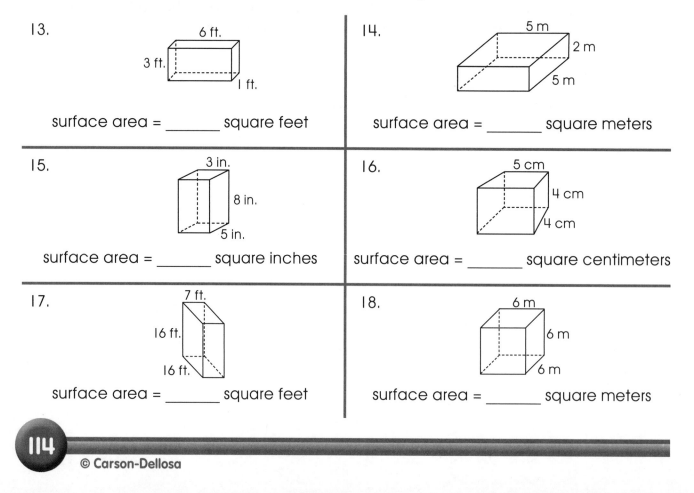

13.

6 ft.

3 ft.

1 ft.

surface area = _____ square feet

14.

5 m

2 m

5 m

surface area = _____ square meters

15.

3 in.

8 in.

5 in.

surface area = _____ square inches

16.

5 cm

4 cm

4 cm

surface area = _____ square centimeters

17.

7 ft.

16 ft.

16 ft.

surface area = _____ square feet

18.

6 m

6 m

6 m

surface area = _____ square meters

Convert each measurement.

16 ounces (oz.) = 1 pound (lb.) 2,000 lb. = 1 ton	2 cups = 1 pint (pt.) 2 pt. = 1 quart (qt.) 8 pt. = 1 gallon (gal.)

1. 32 oz. = _____ lb.

2. 3 lb. = _____ oz.

3. 8 oz. = _____ lb.

4. 4 oz. = _____ lb.

5. 1 ton = _____ lb.

6. 4,000 lb. = _____ tons

7. 2 cups = _____ pt.

8. 3 pt. = _____ cups

9. 2 pt. = _____ qt.

10. 4 qt. = _____ gal.

11. 8 pt. = _____ gal.

12. 1 cup = _____ gal.

Rewrite the friendly letter. Use the correct form, punctuation marks, and capitalization. Be sure to indent each paragraph.

1624 bay lane short creek pa 12525 may 10 2015 dear aunt ann and uncle james school will soon be out for the summer i am looking forward to it the year was good and i learned a lot mom and dad are going to france in july i don't want to go with them I'm writing this letter to ask if i can stay with you july 10 through July 22 i would love to help you take care of the horses and do anything else that you would want me to do i would also help around the house please let me know if i can come your loving niece julie ann

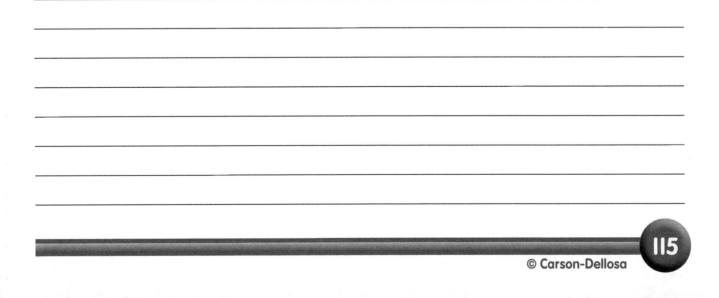

DAY 9

Read the passage. Then, answer the questions.

Gwendolyn Brooks

Gwendolyn Brooks began writing poems when she was seven years old. When her parents saw how much she loved to work with words, they set up a desk for her and told her that she could write instead of doing chores in the house.

Although the Brooks family was poor, they felt rich because they were happy. Later, Brooks wrote about families like hers. These people lived in the city and did not have much money. Sometimes, they did not have enough to eat. In spite of their troubles, they loved life.

By the age of 16, Brooks had published 75 poems. At 25, she won her first writing award. She published her first book of poems, *A Street in Bronzeville*, in 1945. They were poems about people who lived in the part of Chicago, Illinois, where Brooks lived.

In 1949, Brooks published *Annie Allen,* a book of poems for which she won the Pulitzer Prize. Brooks was the first African American to earn this prestigious writing prize. Later, Brooks taught writing at colleges and worked for the Library of Congress.

Brooks wrote some poems about brave people working for equal rights. She wrote about the lives of Southern African Americans as well as life around her in the city. She said that she was like a newspaper writer, reporting the things going on around her.

13. Number the events in the order in which they happened.

_____ Brooks wrote *Annie Allen*.

_____ Brooks's parents set up a desk for her so that she could write.

_____ Brooks published her first book of poems.

_____ Brooks worked for the Library of Congress.

14. What big award did Brooks win? _____

15. Whom did Brooks write about in most of her poems? _____

_____

16. Find several examples of Gwendolyn Brooks's poetry, either online or at the library. What information from the passage above do you find reflected in her poetry? Use a separate sheet of paper if you need additional space to answer.

_____

_____

_____

Convert each measurement.

> 1 liter (L) = 1,000 milliliters (mL)   1 gram (g) = 1,000 milligrams (mg)
> 1 kiloliter (kL) = 1,000 liters (L)   1 kilogram (kg) = 1,000 grams (g)

1. 1,000 mL = _____ L

2. 1,000 L = _____ kL

3. 4 L = _____ mL

4. 5 kL = _____ L

5. 3,000 mL = _____ L

6. 9 L = _____ mL

7. 8 kg = _____ g

8. 4,000 mg = _____ g

9. 9.5 g = _____ mg

10. 2 kg = _____ mg

11. 9,000 g = _____ kg

12. 7 kg = _____ mg

Do you think parents should limit the amount of time that children spend using computers? Make a claim and support it with convincing reasons and evidence.

_____

_____

_____

_____

_____

_____

_____

_____

_____

FITNESS FLASH: Do 10 jumping jacks.

* See page ii.

DAY 10

Write a topic sentence for each paragraph. Try to make each topic sentence interesting so that others will want to read the paragraph.

13. They are among the world's oldest and largest living things. Some are thousands of years old and more than 200 feet (61 m) tall. Some are 100 feet (30.5 m) around at the base. They are the giant sequoia and redwood trees of California and Oregon.

_____

14. It can be a great work, like a Michelangelo carving or an African mask. It can be very large, like the Statue of Liberty, or small enough to place on a table and hold in your hand. It has always played an important part in the history of humanity. Sculpture is an excellent way to express your ideas and feelings.

_____

The rock cycle illustrates three types of changes in rocks. Write the correct phrase from the word bank on each numbered arrow. Each phrase will be used twice.

heating and pressure	melting and crystallization	sedimentation and compaction

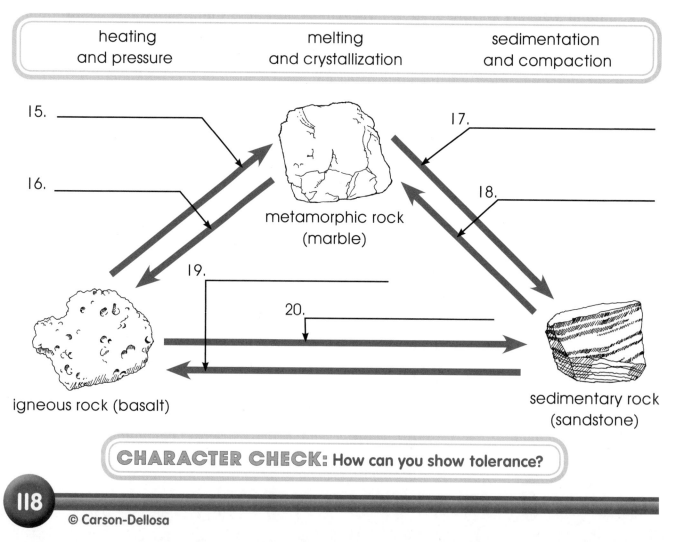

15. _____

16. _____

17. _____

18. _____

19. _____

20. _____

metamorphic rock (marble)

igneous rock (basalt)

sedimentary rock (sandstone)

CHARACTER CHECK: How can you show tolerance?

***Percentage* is the comparison of a number to 100. Write each ratio as a percentage.**

EXAMPLE: $\dfrac{15}{100}$ = **15%**   15 to 100 = **15%**   15:100 = **15%**

1. $\dfrac{20}{100}$ = _____

2. $\dfrac{50}{100}$ = _____

3. 8:100 = _____

4. 47:100 = _____

5. 9 to 100 = _____

Write each percentage as a fraction.

6. 19% = _____

7. 24% = _____

8. 87% = _____

9. 36% = _____

10. 99% = _____

Write each percentage as a fraction. Simplify each fraction.

11. 50% = _____

12. 90% = _____

13. 20% = _____

14. 45% = _____

15. 70% = _____

Sometimes, sentences include additional, non-essential pieces of information about a topic. These *nonrestrictive elements* should be enclosed by a pair of commas, parentheses, or dashes. Rewrite each sentence, including the nonrestrictive element shown below.

16. This year, on my mom's birthday, we will have a family picnic.
     (June 14th)

     _____

17. Jones hit the ball and the crowd went wild.
     —way into left field—

     _____

18. The new puppy got tangled up in her leash.
     , a cocker spaniel,

     _____

DAY II

Context clues help you learn new words and their meanings. Use the context clues in each sentence to tell what the underlined word means.

19. Mary feigned surprise when her friends had a birthday party for her.

_____

20. My colleagues and I work together on many new projects.

_____

21. Maurice looks at his watch often to make sure that he is always punctual.

_____

22. Joseph, a philatelist, has a large collection of stamps.

_____

23. The dog napping in the shade was hardly able to bestir herself for dinner.

_____

The steps describe how a bill becomes a law in the United States. Number the steps in the order in which they happen.

_____ Get the president's approval.

_____ Write a bill.

_____ Get a majority vote in Congress.

_____ If the president vetoes the bill, it may become a law by a two-thirds majority vote in Congress.

Now, create a bill that you think should become a law. Explain why you think that it is needed. On a separate sheet of paper, draw a comic strip that shows characters putting these steps into action.

FACTOID: The great pyramids at Giza were built about 4,500 years ago.

Write each ratio as a fraction.

1. 5 cheetahs to 7 tigers _____

2. 20 tulips to 13 roses _____

3. 12 trumpets to 5 violins _____

4. 4 taxis to 9 buses _____

5. Jill's 23¢ to Bob's 45¢ _____

6. 10 chairs to 3 tables _____

7. 1 meter to 4 meters _____

8. 3 minutes to 25 minutes _____

Use the information in the box to write each ratio as a fraction.

9. soccer balls to footballs _____

10. baseballs to soccer balls _____

11. footballs to baseballs _____

12. baseballs to all balls _____

Circle the noun or verb in parentheses that makes the information in each sentence more specific.

13. Chimpanzees live in (regions, parts) of Africa where jungle vegetation is plentiful.

14. They (hold, grip) tree branches with their palms and long fingers.

15. These (animals, primates) climb trees easily.

16. Chimpanzees eat a variety of foods, including (termites, bugs).

17. If a chimpanzee wants to eat termites, she (pokes, puts) a twig into the center of a termite mound.

18. Then, she removes the twig and (plucks, takes) off the termites.

19. If a male chimpanzee is agitated, he might (run, charge) down a hill, (taking, ripping) off tree branches.

20. He will beat the ground as he (bounds, walks) through the grass.

Read the passage. Then, answer the questions.

Geologists

Geology is the branch of science that deals with Earth's materials and structure. Geologists study processes such as the movement of plates on the planet's crust, volcanic eruptions, and earthquakes. Learning about these events can help scientists predict how Earth might change in the future. Some geologists study the soil to help plants grow better. Farmers can adjust the minerals in their soil to produce bigger crops. Studying water drainage helps scientists learn how to prevent flooding. Some geologists study the makeup of the sea floor, and others research gemstones. Geologists study the movement of glaciers and the use of natural resources, such as oil and gas. Many geologists collect data in the field for weeks or months and return to the laboratory to interpret their data. Geologists can be found in almost every location on Earth.

21. What is the main idea of this passage?
    A. Geologists study the materials and structure of Earth.
    B. Some geologists study the soil to help plants grow better.
    C. Geologists learn about different landforms.

22. What is the author's purpose in writing this selection? Explain your answer.

    _____

    _____

23. Which processes do geologists study? _____

    _____

    _____

24. Why do geologists study soil? _____

    _____

25. What do geologists do in laboratories? _____

    _____

FITNESS FLASH: Jog in place for 30 seconds.

* See page ii.

Bar graphs help you compare data at a glance. Answer the questions about the bar graph.

Valley Fair Music Place kept track of the different types of music it sold during the summer months.

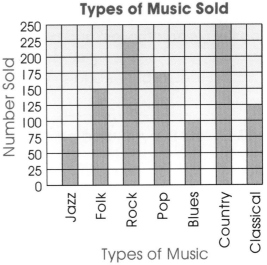

Types of Music Sold

1. Which type of music was the most popular?

   _____

2. Which sold the least? _____

3. What is the difference between the greatest and the least number sold? _____

4. What is the average number of music sold?

   _____

5. Which is your favorite type of music? _____

   _____

Circle the word in parentheses that makes each sentence more descriptive.

6. The concert hall was (big, gigantic).

7. It was (ornately, nicely) decorated in red velvet and gold.

8. The (audience, people) waited eagerly for the concert to begin.

9. The (young, thirty-year-old) conductor raised his baton.

10. The (big, enormous) orchestra came to attention.

11. The audience was (very, completely) still.

12. The orchestra performed (magnificently, well).

13. The tenor sang (nicely, brilliantly).

14. The audience clapped (enthusiastically, loudly).

15. It was a (good, splendid) concert.

FACTOID: Only one percent of Earth's water is drinkable.

DAY 13

Some key words and punctuation marks signal that an author is giving context clues. Write what the underlined word means in each sentence. Then, write the type of signal that helped you determine the word's meaning. Signals include commas, dashes, parentheses, and phrases such as *which is* and *in other words.*

16. I feel <u>torpid</u>—sluggish and lazy—in the hot summer weather.

_____

17. Paul Bunyan used an <u>adze</u>, which is a flat-bladed ax, to cut down the forest.

_____

18. The cook made <u>ragout</u>, a highly seasoned stew, every day for the ranch hands.

_____

19. Jason smashed his <u>patella</u>, in other words, his kneecap.

_____

20. David can play a <u>marimba</u> (a xylophone).

_____

Discovering Perseverance

Perseverance means to keep going even if something is difficult and there are obstacles to overcome. Talk with a family member about the quality of perseverance and discuss friends, family members, or neighbors who have demonstrated this quality in their lives. Then, ask one of the individuals whose name was mentioned if you can conduct an interview with him. During the interview, ask this person specific questions to help you better understand the challenges he overcame to become successful. After the interview, make a three-panel comic strip highlighting a before, a during, and an after scene. In each panel, be sure to include an appropriate quote for that stage of the person's quest: first in getting started, then in never giving up, etc. When the comic strip is completed, schedule a time to meet with the person, sharing the comic strip as well as what you learned from this experience.

FACTOID: Australia's Great Barrier Reef can be seen from outer space.

Pie charts compare parts of a whole. Answer each question about the pie chart.

Jake earns $20 a week doing chores for his neighbors. The pie chart shows how he uses his money.

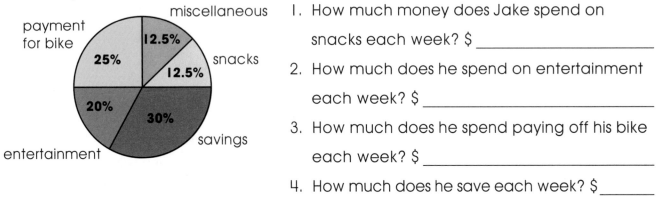

1. How much money does Jake spend on snacks each week? $ _____

2. How much does he spend on entertainment each week? $ _____

3. How much does he spend paying off his bike each week? $ _____

4. How much does he save each week? $ _____

Contractions containing *not* are called *negatives*. Words such as *nothing*, *nobody*, and *never* are also negatives. You should not use double negatives in writing or in speaking. Underline the double negatives in each sentence. Then, rewrite the sentence correctly.

EXAMPLE: The fight <u>didn't</u> solve <u>nothing</u>.

<u>**The fight didn't solve anything.**</u>

5.   The team didn't want no trouble.

   _____

6.   Haven't you never seen Yellowstone National Park?

   _____

7.   There aren't no eggs in the carton.

   _____

8.   He wasn't near no base when he was tagged out.

   _____

9.   There isn't no way to get there from here.

   _____

10.   The explanation didn't make no sense.

   _____

DAY 14

Divide fractions to solve the word problems.

11. A carpenter cuts a board that is $\frac{4}{5}$ meters long into pieces that are $\frac{2}{3}$ meters long. How many pieces will he have?

12. Emil has $8\frac{1}{2}$ ounces of salsa. If he divides it into containers that hold $4\frac{1}{4}$ ounces each, how many containers can he fill?

13. Cara has $\frac{6}{9}$ yard of ribbon. She cuts the ribbon into 3 equal pieces. What is the length of each piece?

14. Adita uses a $4\frac{1}{2}$-pound bag of potting soil to fill 6 pots. How many pounds of soil will be in each pot?

Match each word with its definition. Use a dictionary, a science book, or the Internet if you need help.

15. _____ asteroids

16. _____ comet

17. _____ star

18. _____ satellite

19. _____ planet

A. an object that orbits a planet or a moon

B. rocky or metal objects that orbit the sun in a belt between Mars and Jupiter; also called planetoids or minor planets

C. a huge ball of glowing gas that can exist for billions of years; our sun is the closest one

D. a small object orbiting the sun that is made of frozen ice, gas, and dust; it has a tail that always points away from the sun

E. a large body that orbits a star and does not produce its own light; there are eight in our solar system

FITNESS FLASH: Hop on your left foot 10 times.

* See page ii.

A pictograph uses picture symbols to represent different amounts of data or specific units. Answer each question about the pictograph.

School Visitors

Monday	🚶 🚶 🚶 🚶 🚶 🚶 🚶 🚶
Tuesday	🚶 🚶 🚶 🚶 🚶 🚶
Wednesday	🚶 🚶 🚶
Thursday	🚶 🚶 🚶
Friday	🚶 🚶 🚶 🚶 🚶 🚶

🚶 = 10 family members

Riverton School kept track of how many family members visited their school during Family Week. They made a pictograph to show the students the results.

1. When did most family members visit? _____

2. What does 🚶 mean? _____

3. How many family members visited the school during Family Week? _____

4. When did the least number of family members visit? _____

5. How many family members visited on Friday? _____

6. What other type of graph could have been used to show this data? _____

    _____

Underline the double negatives in each sentence. Then, rewrite the sentence correctly.

7.   Can't no one solve the puzzle? _____

8.   Rick didn't have nothing to read. _____

9.   Annie hadn't never seen that. _____

10. Don't spill none of the juice. _____

11. There isn't nothing you can do about it. _____

    _____

David Glasgow Farragut

At age nine, David Glasgow Farragut went to sea. Farragut's father, who was Spanish, came to the United States in 1776. He fought for his new country in the American Revolution and the War of 1812. Farragut's mother died when he was seven, so he was sent to live with naval captain David Porter. Porter found a place on a ship for Farragut.

Farragut was at sea during the War of 1812. When he was 12 years old, he was put in charge of a prize ship that had been captured from the enemy. Farragut's job was to get the ship safely to port. This was a hard job during a war, but Farragut did it.

After many years of peace, the Civil War began. Farragut loved his home in Virginia, but he told his wife that he was "sticking to the flag." So, the couple moved to New York. David Farragut was 60 years old.

The Mississippi River was guarded too well for the North to use it. Farragut was asked to **capture** New Orleans, Louisiana. It was an important port for the South and the gateway to the huge river system. Farragut took his flagship, the *Hartford*, and almost 50 other ships with him. He captured New Orleans and other cities on the Mississippi. Finally, in 1864, he turned to Mobile, Alabama. Under heavy fire, Farragut captured Mobile, the South's last big port.

In less than two years, the *Hartford* had been hit 240 times by cannon fire. The war was almost over. Farragut went home to New York. Farragut was made an admiral for the important work he did during the Civil War.

12. What does the word *capture* mean in the passage?
    A. to take control of
    B. to guard
    C. to keep safe
    D. to clothe

13. Number the events in the order in which they happened.

    _____ Farragut brought a captured ship safely to port.

    _____ Farragut captured the port of Mobile, Alabama.

    _____ Farragut was sent to live with a navy captain.

    _____ Farragut fought battles on the Mississippi River.

14. What city did Farragut have to capture to get to the Mississippi River? _____

15. What rank was Farragut given at the end of the war? _____

CHARACTER CHECK: Make a list of three things you can do at home that demonstrate cooperation. Share your list with a family member.

Follow the instructions and answer the question.

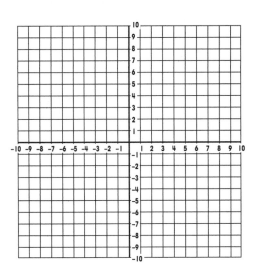

1. Plot point *A* at (−6, 4).

2. Point *B* is at the same distance above the *x*-axis as Point *A*, but it is 10 units away on the opposite side of the *y*-axis. Plot Point *B* and write its coordinates: (_____ , _____).

3. Draw a line connecting *A* and *B*.

4. Plot Point *C* at (8, −4) and draw a line connecting *B* and *C*.

5. Point *D* is at the same distance below the *x*-axis as Point *C*, but it is 17 units away on the opposite side of the *y*-axis. Plot Point *D* and write its coordinates: (_____ , _____).

6. Draw a line connecting *C* and *D*.

7. Draw a line connecting *D* and *A*.

8. What shape have you drawn on the coordinate plane?_____

Correct the paragraph. Draw three lines under each letter that needs to be capitalized. Cross out each misspelled word and write the correct spelling above the word. Add punctuation where needed.

today the term "American Indian" is used to describe people indigenous to america.

however the firt explorers who came to America referred to them as "Indins" unknown

to the explorers, most tribes had their own names. for example the name used by

the deleware indians of eastern north america meant "genuine men." the Indians'

langages ways of life, and homes wer all very different. The aztic and maya Indians

of central america built large citys The apache and Paiute used brushes and mating

to make simple huts the plains indians buit coneshaped tepees covered with buffalo

skns Cliff dwellers and other Pueblo groups usd sun-dried bricks to make many-storyed

houses

DAY 16

Some sentences have clue words or transition words that help show cause-and-effect relationships. Complete each sentence with a clue word or transition word. Then, write the cause and effect.

EXAMPLE: Our school was closed today <u>because</u> of the snowstorm we had last night.

Cause: **snowstorm**

Effect: **school was closed**

9. It snowed all day, _____ the ground was white.

Cause: _____

Effect: _____

10. Our electricity went out last night, _____ we went out to dinner.

Cause: _____

Effect: _____

11. Joe left the gate unlatched, _____ all of the cattle were out in the road.

Cause: _____

Effect: _____

12. Scott woke up with the flu today, _____ he had to miss school.

Cause: _____

Effect: _____

Pollution is a problem that affects all living things on Earth. Match each term with its description.

13. _____ leaked oil from a tanker that ran aground   A. greenhouse effect

14. _____ poisonous materials such as paint thinner   B. hazardous waste

15. _____ smoke and exhaust that mix with water vapor   C. acid rain

16. _____ a warming of the surface and lower atmosphere of Earth   D. oil spill

FACTOID: Hummingbirds can fly up to 60 miles (96.5 km) per hour.

Write the integer for each letter on the number line.

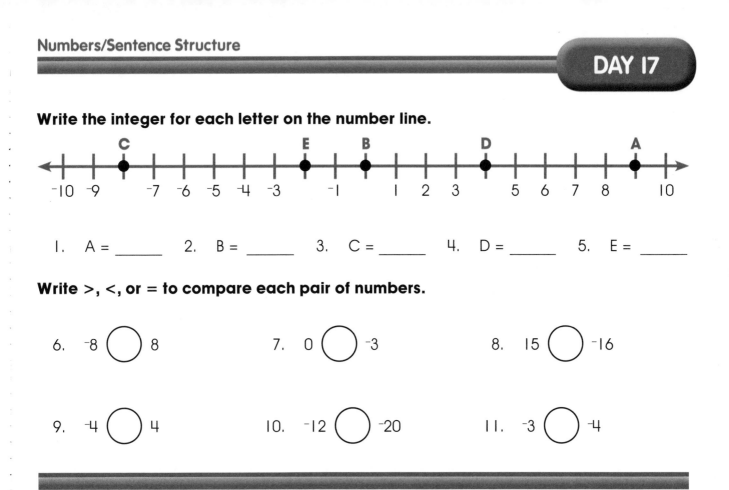

1. A = _____   2. B = _____   3. C = _____   4. D = _____   5. E = _____

Write >, <, or = to compare each pair of numbers.

6. ⁻8 ◯ 8   7. 0 ◯ ⁻3   8. 15 ◯ ⁻16

9. ⁻4 ◯ 4   10. ⁻12 ◯ ⁻20   11. ⁻3 ◯ ⁻4

Use the common predicates or subjects in each group of sentences to write a single sentence.

12. Jim liked to visit Grandma and Grandpa. Sean liked to visit Grandma and Grandpa. Maria liked to visit Grandma and Grandpa.

_____

_____

13. Grandpa had horses on his farm. Grandpa had cows on his farm. Grandpa had goats on his farm.

_____

_____

14. Grandma raised chickens. Grandma raised ducks. Grandma raised geese.

_____

15. Daisies grew in her garden. Tulips grew in her garden. Roses grew in her garden.

_____

DAY 17

Write an effect to complete each sentence. Look for clue words or transition words.

EXAMPLE: The old house had not been painted in years,
so <u>the first thing we did was paint it</u>.

16. The oven temperature was too high, so _____ .

17. _____ because my new shoes were too tight.

18. The wind was blowing hard, so _____ .

19. Because I didn't get up early enough this morning, _____ .

20. _____ because I didn't study.

Write a cause to complete each sentence.

21. The plane was delayed due to _____ .

22. _____ , so my stomach hurt.

23. _____ , so we decided to celebrate.

24. The drinks were very sweet because _____ .

25. _____ , so there was no fruit on the trees this summer.

Skip to Success!

Skipping is a great way to build endurance and improve your speed, agility, and quickness. Find a long, flat surface, such as a sidewalk, driveway, or yard. To begin, skip forward, lifting one knee forward and into the air. At the same time, raise your opposite arm. Concentrate on jumping straight into the air and reaching your arms as high as possible. Skip for 30 seconds, alternating legs. Repeat this 3–5 times. To make this activity more challenging, try skipping for longer periods of time or increasing your number of repetitions.

FITNESS FLASH: Hop on your right foot for 30 seconds.

Use the Venn diagram to compare each set of data.

1. Mark, Heather, and Charita compared the multiples of 4 and 5.
   Multiples of 4: 0, 4, 8, 12, 16, 20
   Multiples of 5: 0, 5, 10, 15, 20, 25

2. Cameron, Sean, and Alexandra compared the diameters of the seeds they found.
   Cameron: 0.5 cm, 1 cm, 1.5 cm, 2 cm
   Sean: 0.5 cm, 1.5 cm, 3 cm, 3.5 cm
   Alexandra: 0.25 cm, 0.5 cm, 2 cm, 3 cm

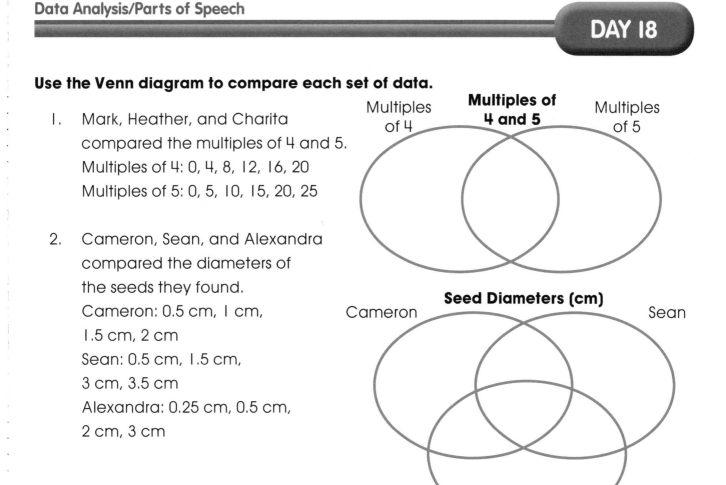

Circle the possessive pronoun that correctly completes each sentence.

EXAMPLE:

Maggie collects books, and she likes (her, she) old books best.

3. Ty said that (he, his) parents also collect books.

4. Emily washed (her, hers) hair.

5. I asked (my, mine) sister to give me a ride home.

6. The cat bathed (hers, her) kittens.

7. The girls made lunch for (their, theirs) family.

8. "Craig, please write (yours, your) phone number on the sign-up sheet."

DAY 18

Read the poem. Then, answer the questions.

The Road Not Taken by Robert Frost

Two roads diverged in a yellow wood,
And sorry I could not travel both
And be one traveler, long I stood
And looked down one as far as I could
To where it bent in the undergrowth;

Then took the other, as just as fair,
And having perhaps the better claim,
Because it was grassy and wanted wear;
Though as for that the passing there
Had worn them really about the same,

And both that morning equally lay
In leaves no step had trodden black.
Oh, I kept the first for another day!
Yet knowing how way leads on to way,
I doubted if I should ever come back.

I shall be telling this with a sigh
Somewhere ages and ages hence:
Two roads diverged in a wood, and I—
I took the one less traveled by,
And that has made all the difference.

9. After you read the poem, visit the following Web site: www.poets.org/poetsorg/ poem/road-not-taken. Listen to Robert Frost read the poem himself. How is your experience listening to the poet read the poem different than reading it yourself? Use a separate sheet of paper if necessary for your answer.

_____

_____

10. What is the main idea of this poem?

_____

_____

11. Reread the last stanza of the poem. How does it bring the poem to a

conclusion? _____

_____

Follow the directions for the coordinate graph.

1. Plot each coordinate pair and label each point. The first one has been done for you.

(2, 2) A	(12, 8) L
(12, 16) H	(8, 10) D
(16, 12) J	(10, 8) N
(6, 4) P	(13, 13) I
(14, 10) K	(6, 8) C
(10, 14) G	(10, 11) E
(4, 6) B	(11, 10) M
(8, 12) F	
(8, 6) O	

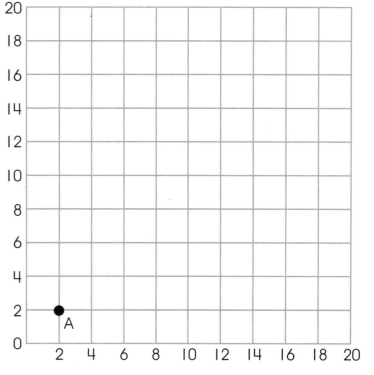

2. Connect points A through P in alphabetical order.

3. Connect point P to point A.

4. Connect point E to point I and point I to point M.

The pronouns *who* and *whom* can be used to ask a question or introduce a clause. *Who* is used when the pronoun is the subject. *Whom* is used when the pronoun is an object. Write *who* or *whom* to complete each sentence.

5. _____ made the first moon landing?

6. _____ do you like the best among the candidates?

7. _____ is your best friend?

8. _____ won the gold medal?

9. _____ does Ryan think will be the best choice for the math contest?

10. _____ was the man she saw walking his dog?

11. _____ shall I call in case of an emergency?

12. He is the person _____ is always late!

13. One of the boys _____ we know is very tall.

14. A teacher _____ we admire spoke at our graduation.

DAY 19

Underline the noun that is being personified in each sentence. Then, write the personifying word or words.

15. The first-place trophy proudly stood on the shelf in Charlie's room.

    _____

16. Because we could not go out to play, we watched from our window as the clouds spit icicles.

    _____

17. Autumn leaves seemed to sing as they danced across the lawn.

    _____

18. Horns honked angrily as drivers became impatient.

    _____

19. The sun played hide-and-seek with me as it popped in and out of the clouds.

    _____

Because of women like Lucy Stone, Susan B. Anthony, Lucretia Mott, Elizabeth Cady Stanton, and Sarah and Angelina Grimké, women in the United States have many rights today that they didn't have in earlier times. Research one of these women and write an essay about the trials she had to go through because of what she believed.

_____

_____

_____

_____

_____

_____

_____

_____

FITNESS FLASH: Do 10 jumping jacks.

* See page ii.

Box plots are used to determine the distribution of data. Look at the example below. The results of a test might include these 15 scores: 48, 56, 65, 66, 72, 73, 74, 75, 77, 81, 83, 85, 87, 89, 98. Make sure the data is arranged in numerical order. Then, plot the *median* (75) on a number line. The *lower quartile* is the median of the lower half (66). The *upper quartile* is the median of the upper half (85). Draw a box around the median with its ends going through the quartiles. Each quartile contains one-fourth of the scores. Some people call this type of graph a *box-and-whisker plot*. The "whiskers" are the two lines extending to the highest and lowest values of the data.

EXAMPLE:

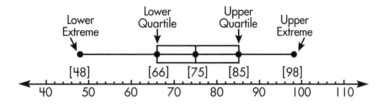

1. Using the number line below, draw a box plot for these scores: 10, 15, 15, 20, 20, 25, 30, 30, 35, 40, 40.

    0   5   10   15   20   25   30   35   40   45   50

2. What is the median score? _____

3. What is the lower quartile? _____

4. What is the upper quartile? _____

The verb *can* is used to express mental or physical ability. *May* is used to express possibility or ask permission. The verb *lie* means to rest or recline. The verb *lay* means to put or place something. Circle the verb that correctly completes each sentence.

5. Bingo, (lie, lay) down!

6. Toto (may, can) do several tricks, such as sitting, shaking, and rolling over.

7. Mom, (may, can) Amy spend the night on Friday?

8. No one (may, can) understand the problem like Evelyn!

9. Janie (may, can) return to work when she is feeling well again.

10. Please (lie, lay) the paper on the stairs.

DAY 20

Circle the mood of each sentence.

11. The grayish clouds overshadowed the day.
   A. happy
   B. sad
   C. quiet

12. Larry looked toward the ground and tried to hold back his tears.
   A. happy
   B. sad
   C. quiet

13. As the waves slowly touched the shore, the water whispered softly.
   A. happy
   B. sad
   C. quiet

14. The clown's bright costume jiggled as he played with the perky puppy.
   A. happy
   B. sad
   C. quiet

15. The children's laughter floated through the air as they splashed in the pool.
   A. happy
   B. sad
   C. quiet

16. A hushed silence fell over the crowd.
   A. happy
   B. sad
   C. quiet

Match each inventor with his invention. Use the Internet if you need help.

17. _____ Eli Whitney

18. _____ Elias Howe

19. _____ Levi Strauss

20. _____ Cyrus McCormick

21. _____ Samuel F. B. Morse

22. _____ Thomas Edison

23. _____ Alexander G. Bell

A. telegraph

B. phonograph

C. sewing machine

D. cotton gin

E. telephone

F. reaper

G. blue jeans

CHARACTER CHECK: Write down three good things that you are going to do today and do them!

How Do Lungs Work?

Have you ever wondered how your lungs are able to breathe in and out? In this activity, you will learn about how lungs work.

Materials
- balloons (2 small, 1 large)
- 2-liter plastic bottle
- masking tape
- rubber bands (small and large)
- 2 pipettes
- rubber tubing
- scissors

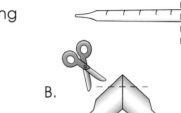

Procedure
1. Cut the pipettes (A). You may need an adult's help.
2. Place the pipette bulbs together and hold them together with tape. Then, cut off the tops of the bulbs, creating a "Y" connector (B).
3. Insert your new Y-shaped piece into the rubber tubing and tape it in place. Attach the two small balloons to the arms of the "Y" with small rubber bands.
4. Have an adult help you cut off the bottom of the 2-liter bottle.
5. Insert the tubing through the bottom of the bottle and out through the neck. Use tape to seal the tubing at the neck so that the balloons are suspended inside the bottle.
6. Cut the neck off the large balloon. Stretch the rest of the balloon over the bottom of the bottle. Use a large rubber band to keep it in place.
7. Pull on the bottom of the balloon, being careful not to pull it off the bottle. Watch what happens to the small balloons.

What's This All About?
The long tube at the top represents your trachea, where the air comes in. The two arms of the plastic piece represent bronchial tubes, which lead to the lungs. The small balloons are the lungs. By pulling on the bottom balloon, which represents the diaphragm (a large muscle under the lungs), you lower the pressure inside the bottle (your chest cavity). This causes the "lungs" to inflate because the outside air pressure is now higher than the inside air pressure and air rushes in to equalize it. When you let go of the diaphragm, you increase the inside air pressure and the lungs deflate as the air rushes out. The diaphragm (with help from other muscles) pulls air into the lungs and pushes it out again. While the air is inside, the lungs collect carbon dioxide from the blood and put oxygen back into it. The carbon dioxide is then pushed out with the next exhale.

* See page ii.

BONUS

All About Backbones

Where would you be without a backbone? You wouldn't be able to pick up your pencil if you dropped it. You wouldn't be able to walk. You wouldn't even be able to sit in a chair. Without a backbone, you wouldn't be able to do much of anything!

Materials

- 11 cardboard tubes (short)
- 11 rubber bands (1 inch long)
- hole punch
- scissors

Procedure

1. Cut each cardboard tube into thirds. If the tubes bend as you cut them, push them back to their original shapes.
2. Punch two holes on opposite sides of each tube section. Use the top illustration as a guide.
3. Loop the rubber bands together to form one long string. Thread the string of rubber bands through the holes in the tube sections one at a time. When all of the sections are threaded on the rubber-band string, tie off the string at the top and bottom.
4. Experiment by bending your handmade backbone in different directions. See if your backbone has limitations. Try to figure out what would happen if one or more sections were damaged or had to be removed.
5. Imagine that your real backbone is frozen into one solid piece for 60 seconds. Demonstrate how you would walk across the room, pick up a chair, and put it down again. Remember, none of your vertebrae can move for 60 seconds.

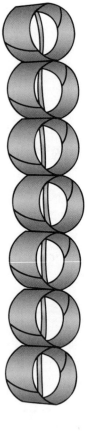

What's This All About?

The backbone serves as the major supporting structure in the body, so it must possess great rigidity. At the same time, it must be flexible enough to allow twisting, turning, and bending. To accommodate this movement, the backbone is divided into sections called *vertebrae*. The human body has 33 vertebrae. They permit swaying and bending and, at the same time, provide support for the head and places for the ribs to attach. Additionally, the delicate spinal cord runs through these vertebrae, with each vertebra providing openings or exit points where the spinal nerves can go to the various organs in the body.

Governing a Nation

The United States Constitution is organized into seven sections called *articles*. The articles are numbered with Roman numerals. Match each article with its summary. Use an encyclopedia, the Internet, or another reference if you need help.

1. _____ Article I

2. _____ Article II

3. _____ Article III

4. _____ Article IV

5. _____ Article V

6. _____ Article VI

7. _____ Article VII

A. says that at least nine states must accept the Constitution before it can become a law

B. states that the Constitution is the law of the land and that all senators and representatives must swear to support the Constitution

C. describes the powers of the Supreme Court and other federal courts

D. describes how the president will be elected, who can run for president, and what powers and responsibilities the president has

E. describes how the states will relate to each other, how new states can be added to the Union, and how the federal government will protect the states

F. describes how amendments, or changes, can be made to the Constitution

G. describes how Congress will be set up, how laws will be made, and what powers Congress will have

Read each description of Canada's system of government. Then, fill in the blanks to complete each description of the U.S. government.

8. Canada is comprised of 10 provinces and three territories. The United States is comprised of _____ states, the _____ of Columbia, and territories.

9. Canada is a parliamentary democracy and a constitutional monarchy, with a king or queen of England as its head of state. The United States is a constitutional _____ with a _____ as its head of state.

10. Each province in Canada has its own legislature and is governed by a federally appointed commissioner. Each U.S. state has its own _____ and is governed by a _____ .

BONUS

United States Supreme Court

Read the passage. Then, circle *yes* or *no* to answer each question.

The U.S. Supreme Court is the highest court in the country. Its main job is to rule on cases that involve questions about laws in the Constitution. The Supreme Court also has the last say in cases that have gone through the lower courts. The Supreme Court is not like a trial court. Instead of one judge, there are nine, and there is no jury of U.S. citizens to make the decisions. The judges make the final decisions, called *rulings*. The Supreme Court cannot make new laws, but their rulings are similar to laws because all other courts must follow their decisions. The judges on the U.S. Supreme Court are called *justices*. Supreme Court justices are chosen by the president of the United States with approval from the Senate. After a judge is chosen as a Supreme Court justice, he or she has the job for life.

1. Can another court change the decision of a Supreme Court case?

   yes   no

2. Does the Supreme Court use a jury to make decisions?

   yes   no

3. Do other courts have to follow Supreme Court rulings?

   yes   no

4. Is there more than one judge on the Supreme Court?

   yes   no

5. Does the U.S. Senate choose the Supreme Court justices?

   yes   no

6. Does a Supreme Court justice lose his or her job after 10 years?

   yes   no

7. Can the Supreme Court write new laws?

   yes   no

8. Does the Supreme Court settle questions about the Constitution?

   yes   no

Research the current Supreme Court justices and write their names on a separate sheet of paper.

The States

Read the passage. Then, circle *true* or *false* for each statement.

From Alaska to Hawaii and California to Maine, the states of the United States have such different concerns that federal laws cannot meet each state's specific needs. State government allows each state to make rules and laws that are specific to its state. Each state has a capital city (like the country's capital, Washington, D.C.) where the government does its work. The organization of state government is similar to the organization of the federal government. Each state in the United States has an executive, a legislative, and a judicial branch of government. The executive branch in state government is headed by the state's governor. The legislative branch in all state governments except Nebraska has an upper house (usually called a senate) and a lower house (usually called a house of representatives) to make laws. (Nebraska has just one state house.) The judicial branch in state government contains state courts and a state supreme court. Each state also has its own constitution. One state's constitution and laws can be very different from another's but cannot go against the U.S. Constitution.

1.	Each state's constitution is the same.	true	false
2.	Each state has three branches of government.	true	false
3.	Every state has two houses in the legislative branch.	true	false
4.	Every state has a governor.	true	false
5.	A state's constitution can keep women from voting in that state.	true	false
6.	A governor is to a state as the president is to the country.	true	false
7.	State governments do their work in Washington, D.C.	true	false
8.	Federal laws are not specific enough to meet all states' needs.	true	false
9.	Each state has a supreme court.	true	false
10.	The executive branch makes the laws in state government.	true	false

BONUS

Take It Outside!

Take a pen and a notebook and walk around your neighborhood. Pay special attention to street signs, house numbers, and building addresses. When you find a number, write it in your notebook. Make a list of all of the numbers you see. Then, rewrite all of the numbers as Roman numerals. Share the Roman numeral results with your friends and neighbors. Do they recognize the addresses written as Roman numerals?

Take a pen and a notebook outside and find a place to sit. Look around and observe what you see and hear. Identify something near where you are sitting, such as a tree, a bench, or a stream, that is a permanent feature. Imagine how this object might view the experiences of a typical day. Then, write a letter from the object's perspective to the people who pass by it every day.

With a family member, identify two parks in your community. Take a pen and a notebook and visit both parks. Make a list of what you find in each park. After your visits, review what is on your lists, noting what is on both lists and what appears on just one list. Next, use this information to create a Venn diagram that shows how the two parks are alike and how they are different.

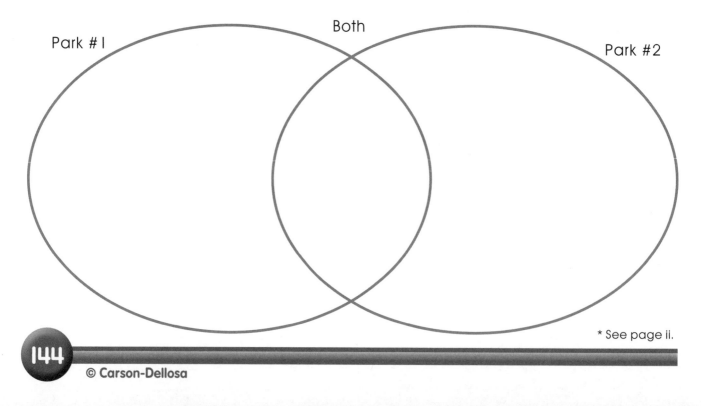

Park #1   Both   Park #2

* See page ii.

Section I

Day 1/Page 3: 1. 21,411; 2. 84,525; 3. 892; 4. 519,549; 5. 1,212; 6. 66 R4; 7. 42,094; 8. $1,668.41; 9. 71,130; 10. 12,848; 11. B; 12. A; 13. B; 14. A; 15.–24. Answers will vary.; 25. 120; 26. 15; 27. 23; 28. 72; 29. 6; 30. 4; 31. 65; 32. 300; 33. 128; 34. 50; 35. 520; 36. 2,502

Day 2/Page 5: 1. 2,685,322; 2. 478.53; 3. 23,409,036; 4. 2,111.097; 5. 304.804; 6. 16,053,245.99; 7. (3 × 10,000,000) + (7 × 1,000,000) + (1 × 100,000) + (2 × 10,000) + (6 × 1,000) + (4 × 100) + (8 × 10) + (9 × 1) + (2 × $\frac{1}{10}$); 8. (2 × 1,000) + (6 × 10) + (9 × 1) + (4 × $\frac{1}{100}$) + (4 × $\frac{1}{1000}$); 9. for; 10. about; 11. on; 12. into; 13. to; 14. beyond; 15. after; 16. in; 17. to; 18. into, at; 19. camping; 20. packed; 21. hunt; 22. picked; 23. Parking; 24. splashing; 25. Anchorage; 26. Los Angeles; 27. Kansas City; 28. New Orleans; 29. Detroit; 30. Ottawa; 31. Albuquerque; 32. New York City; 33. Columbus; 34. Calgary

Day 3/Page 7: work, selects, go, like, choose, take, grab, sit, have, finish, share, meet, explains, answers, enjoy; 1. spice, Variety makes life interesting.; 2. cake, You can't have everything you want.; 3. basket, Don't count on any one thing.; 4. leap, Think about what you are going to do before you do it.; 5. turn, When you do something kind for someone, they will return the favor.; 6. The Lunar Module had landed on the moon.; 7. moon; 8. because the astronauts might not get another chance to go to the moon or to return to *Apollo 11*; 9. They were the first people to walk on the moon.; 10. Answers will vary.

Day 4/Page 9: 1. A, C, E, F, H, I,; 2. E, J; 3. A, B; 4. E, F, H; 5. A, G; 6. D, E; 7. B; 8. C, E, F; 9. <u>geo</u>graphy; 10. transport<u>ation</u>; 11. ex<u>tract</u>; 12. meteor<u>ology</u>; 13. <u>derma</u>tology; 14. <u>December</u>; 15.–26. Answers will vary.; Students' writing will vary.

Day 5/Page 11: 1. 5; 2. 9; 3. 4; 4. 6; 5. 2; 6. 8; 7. both, and; 8. Just as, so; 9. Neither, nor; 10. either, or; 11. not only, but; 12. Neither, nor; 13. Either,

or; 14. Whether, or; 15. Both, and; 16. either, or; 17. the act of punishing; 18. vanish; 19. to soak before; 20. to wind again; 21. without color; 22. cooked before; 23. not sure; 24. like brown

Day 6/Page 13: 1. 7$\frac{5}{8}$; 2. 2$\frac{4}{45}$; 3. 4$\frac{1}{12}$; 4. 12$\frac{13}{40}$; 5. 3$\frac{4}{21}$; 6. $\frac{17}{40}$; 7. 5$\frac{7}{12}$; 8. 1$\frac{1}{2}$; 9. 1$\frac{1}{3}$; 10. 7$\frac{1}{2}$; 11. 2$\frac{5}{8}$; 12. 96; 13. 4$\frac{19}{20}$; 14. $\frac{1}{36}$; 15. $\frac{1}{20}$; 16.–19. Answers will vary.; 20. C.; 21. an ecosystem; 22. Answers may include: grasslands, wetlands, tundra, mountain, maritime, temperate rain forests, temperate deciduous forests.; 23. permafrost; 24. It is near the Atlantic Ocean.; 25. the Hudson Plains; 26. the sea; 27. Paragraphs will vary.

Day 7/Page 15: 1. 28.875; 2. 661; 3. 123.773; 4. 98.5; 5. 9; 6. 184.6; 7. 99.333; 8. 83.2; Book reviews will vary.; 9. G; 10. I; 11. C; 12. H; 13. B; 14. D; 15. F; 16. J; 17. E; 18. A; 19. 45 years; 20. 27 years; 21. 18 years; 22. 48 years

Day 8/Page 17: 1. 1$\frac{7}{15}$ pounds; 2. 6$\frac{13}{84}$ feet tall; 3. 2$\frac{17}{60}$ hours; 4. 1$\frac{7}{40}$ hours; Circled verbs include: walk, sound, call, dance, sit, caught, honked, smell, plays, wore, gather, throw, jump, won, dive, rolled, wiggled, sneezed, read, eat, cheer, meowing, barking, selling, climbs, skiing, paint, cry, built, speak, carried, bake, wash, practice, blew, clapped, watched, wants, mopped, hit, helped, carried, fed.; Underlined verbs include: are, be, been, seem, being, will, were, is, am, become, have been, was, has, has had, became, have, had.; 5. stethoscope; 6. suspicious; 7. subscribe; 8. margin; 9. owes; 10. frank; 11. knead; 12. allergies; 13. conduct; 14. inlets; Solids: box, dust, rock, ice; Liquids: juice, lava, milk, water; Gases: air, helium, hydrogen, oxygen

Day 9/Page 19: 1. 0.7; 2. 160; 3. 92; 4. 8,000; 5. 25; 6. 4,200; 7. 100; 8. 4,500; 9. 4.2; 10. 12,000; 11. 60; 12. 240,000; 13. 8,000; 14. 2,700; 15. 150,000; 16.

am; 17. is; 18. were; 19. was; 20. Are; 21. has been; 22. is being; 23. will be; 24.–27. Answers will vary.; 28. North Carolina; 29. four years; 30. Answers will vary.; 31. Students' letters will vary.

Day 10/Page 21: 1. 38,822; 2. 16,936; 3. 15,687; 4. 49,623; 5. 172,072; 6. 288,357; 7. 90,741; 8. 457,666; 9. rang; 10. built; 11. fed; 12. chose; 13. spent; 14. spun; 15. ran; 16. awoke; 17. became; 18. brought; 19. drew; 20. grew; 21. OK,; 22. Shh!; 23. Ouch,; 24. Wow!; 25. Mmmm,; 26. Really,; 27. Stop!; 28. Hold on,; 29. Oops!; 30. Hey,

Day 11/Page 23: 1. 42; 2. 72; 3. 25; 4. 55; 5. 24; 6. 54; 7. 0; 8. 54; 9. 50; 10. 110; 11. 27; 12. 108; 13. 36; 14. 90; 15. 28; 16. 48; 17. 56; 18. 99; 19. 48; 20. 70; 21. 132; 22. 21; 23. 81; 24. 55; 25. 35; 26. 120; 27. 63; 28. 100; 29. 22; 30. 72; 31. 40; 32. 66; 33. 30; 34. 64; 35. 40; 36. 132; 37. ate; 38. shook; 39. held; 40. bled; 41. wrote; 42. rode; 43. taught; 44. fought; 45. froze; 46. (84 ÷ 12) + 16; 47. (12 × 7) – 14; 48. (63 ÷ 9) × 7; 49. (54 – 32) × (8 – 5); 50. (36 ÷ 3) × (15 – 2); 51. (28 – 4) ÷ 6; 52. proprietor; 53. cash crops; 54. indigo; 55. indentured servants

Day 12/Page 25: 1. 125 cm³; 2. 8 ft.³; 3. 343 yd.³; 4. 1,000 mm³; 5. 1,728 in.³; 6. 1 m³; 7. Answers will include: swim, ring, sing, see, begin, eat, go.; 8. Answers will include: swam, rang, sang, saw, began, ate, went.; 9. Answers will include: swum, rung, sung, seen, begun, eaten, gone.; 10. remodel; 11. deposit; 12. giggle; 13. shelves; 14. penalty; 15. predict; 16. precise; 17. estimate; 18. business; 19. giant; Students' writing will vary.

Day 13/Page 27:

Point	x	y	(x, y)
A	1	3	(1, 3)
B	2	4	(2, 4)
C	3	5	(3, 5)
D	4	6	(4, 6)
E	5	7	(5, 7)
F	6	8	(6, 8)
G	7	9	(7, 9)

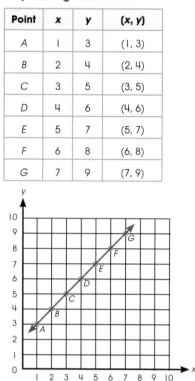

1. will build; 2. will check; 3. will map; 4. will board; 5. will count; 6. will launch; 7. will view; 8. will observe; 9. will record; 10. will photograph; 11. 4; 12. Precambrian, Paleozoic, Mesozoic, Cenozoic; 13. Mesozoic; 14. 3; 15. Triassic, Jurassic, Cretaceous; 16. Cenozoic

Day 14/Page 29: 1. jumbo; 2. 6 dozen small eggs; 3. large; 4. 72, small; 5. 120 ounces; 6. Stargirl; 7. The Wizard of Oz; 8. Walk Two Moons, Wonder; 9. Grease, "Summer Nights"; 10. Peter Pan; 11. "The Red Wheelbarrow"; 12. "The Wheels on the Bus"; 13. Star Wars; 14. Modern Family; Febuary February, Journel Journal, definately definitely, calender calendar, naybor neighbor, suprised surprised, cuboards cupboards, vacume vacuum, your you're, especialy especially, priviledge privilege, untill until; Questions will vary.

Day 15/Page 31: 1. 249$\frac{1}{2}$ ml; 2. 644 ml; 3. 64$\frac{2}{5}$ ml; 4. 56 ml; 5. Answers will vary. Possible answer:

asparagus; 6. between *dilute* and *julienne*; 7. julienne; 8. a pot roast; 9.–18. Answers will vary.

Day 16/Page 33: 1. use; 2. propels; 3. are; 4. dig; 5. carries; 6. enjoy; 7. steers; 8. is; Students should circle the words in green: 9. wild, eerie, **wind**; 10. fuzzy, brown, **caterpillar**; 11. fresh, cool, **water**; 12. hot, tired, **explorers**; large, clear, **lake**; 13. spicy, **aroma**; apple, **cider**; Jason's, small, warm, **tent**; 14. longest; 15. wider; 16. youngest; 17. largest; 18. smaller; 19. seeping into, filling; 20. *he scraped and scratched and scrabbled and scrooged and then he scrooged again and scrabbled and scratched and scraped,* Answers will vary. Possible answer: The repeated sounds of the words are similar to the mole's motions as he digs. Alliteration makes the description more interesting to read.; 21. Answers will vary. Possible answer: Grahame shows how busy the mole is and how hard he is working. Grahame also shows the reader that even though the mole is industrious, he is willing to give up his cleaning to enjoy the spring day.

Day 17/Page 35: 1. 2$\frac{1}{8}$ hours; 2. 2$\frac{8}{15}$ pounds; 3. 2$\frac{7}{12}$ cups; 4. 8$\frac{5}{24}$ miles; 5. PA; 6. PN; 7. PA; 8. PN; 9. PA; 10. PA; 11. PN; 12. PA; 13. PA, PA; **Across:** 2. smart, 3. great, 4. chew, 5. remember, 6. doctor, **Down:** 1. wellknown (well-known), 2. starving, 3. grabbed, 4. crowd; 2, 1, 5, 6, 7, 4, 3

Day 18/Page 37: 1. 2$\frac{3}{8}$ cups of dry pasta; 2. 19$\frac{1}{4}$ inches; 3. 40 napkins; 4. 18 cups of tea; 5.–7. Order of answers may vary. 5. immediately, lately, never, often, soon, today; 6. carefully, eagerly, hard, quickly, softly, wildly; 7. above, far, here, inside, there, upstairs; 8. moist; 9. enclosed; 10. ignorant; 11. freeze; 12. valuable; 13. outer core, inner core; 14. mantle; 15. lithosphere; 16. core; 17. center of Earth

Day 19/Page 39: 1. 1$\frac{1}{8}$; 2. 1$\frac{5}{42}$; 3. $\frac{1}{4}$; 4. 2$\frac{11}{14}$; 5. 1$\frac{11}{12}$; 6. $\frac{21}{22}$; 7. 3$\frac{5}{6}$; 8. 3$\frac{3}{8}$; 9. $\frac{24}{91}$; 10. <; 11. =; 12. >; 13.

<; 14. =; 15. =; 16. <; 17. <; 18. =; 19. had explained; 20. had tried; 21. has visited; 22. will have returned; 23. has been excited; 24. will have played; 25. had hoped; 26. will have read; 27. A.; 28. Answers may include: Olympic Games, democracy, statues, buildings, medical texts, trade routes, epic poetry; 29. Modern sports arenas are based on ancient Greek stadiums.; 30. The author explains facts about Greek contributions to medicine, trade routes, and poetry.; 31. Their medical texts were used for hundreds of years.

Day 20/Page 41: 1. 6; 2. 10; 3. 5; 4. 16; 5. 48; 6. 12; 7. 15; 8. 21; 9. 48; 10. 15; 11. 60; 12. 9; 13. 45; 14. 20; 15. 15; 16. 96; 17. Meanwhile, Mom and Dad wrapped Diego's gifts.; 18. After the storm had blown over, Grandpa went outside to survey the damage.; 19. You haven't locked your keys in the car, have you?; 20. Yes, I think the outfit you're wearing is appropriate for the recital.; 21. Furthermore, you didn't do any of your chores this week.; 22. Did you remember to lock the back door, Danny?; 23. Next, mix the milk, oil, and egg into the dry ingredients.; 24. Dr. Alonzo, have you received the results of the tests yet?; 25. On Wednesday morning, Tara has an orthodontist appointment.; 26. Although Liam was pleased with the final results of his art project, he had struggled a bit in the beginning.; 27. Mrs. Antonelli doesn't know the Rockwell twins, does she?; 28. enjoys; 29. destroy; 30. often; 31. foolish; 32. reality; 33. 5.7; 34. 0.4; 35. 2.4; 36. 3.0; 37. 8.5; 38. 0.9; 39. 6.0; 40. 6.0; 41. 2.15; 42. 0.95; 43. 3.25; 44. 9.89; 45. 7.11; 46. 5.01; 47. 1.25; 48. 2.46

Bonus Page 46: 1. s.; 2. F.; 3. i.; 4. J.; 5. q.; 6. L.; 7. c.; 8. H.; 9. x.; 10. X.; 11. b.; 12. S.; 13. h.; 14. K.; 15. j.; 16. P.; 17. r.; 18. W.; 19. t.; 20. D.; 21. o.; 22. B.; 23. g.; 24. U.; 25. y.; 26. N.; 27. d.; 28. I.; 29. w.; 30. R.; 31. m.; 32. T.; 33. u.; 34. C.; 35. e.; 36. M.; 37. n.; 38. G.; 39. k.; 40. V.; 41. p.; 42. E.; 43. v.; 44. A.; 45. a.; 46. Q.; 47. l.; 48. Y.; 49. f.; 50. O

Section II

Day 1/Page 51: 1. $9\frac{1}{3}$; 2. $3\frac{1}{2}$; 3. $4\frac{3}{4}$; 4. $6\frac{1}{2}$; 5. $4\frac{1}{2}$; 6. 7; 7. $2\frac{1}{3}$; 8. $1\frac{1}{4}$; 9. 4; 10. 8; 11. 16; 12. 36; 13. no; 14. no; 15. yes; 16. Commas are inserted after: Debbie, Don,; 17. business, cultural,; 18. Bronx, Manhattan, Queens, Brooklyn,; 19. Chinatown, Greenwich Village,; 20. Square, Center,; 21.–30. Answers will vary.; 31. It has a magnetic field.; 32. the north and south poles; 33. by studying the magnetic particles within rocks

Day 2/Page 53: 1.–10. Pictures will vary, but actual answers include: 1. $\frac{3}{8}$; 2. $\frac{1}{8}$; 3. $\frac{1}{6}$; 4. $\frac{2}{9}$; 5. $\frac{1}{9}$; 6. $\frac{1}{12}$; 7. $\frac{8}{15}$; 8. $\frac{4}{9}$; 9. $\frac{1}{6}$; 10. $\frac{3}{10}$; 11. However; 12. Although; 13. in addition; 14. nevertheless; 15. Moreover; 16. Similarly; 17. C.; 18. about 3,500 years (from 2600 BC to AD 900); 19. Guatemala, Belize, El Salvador, parts of Honduras and southeast Mexico; 20. It had 260 days with a festival every 20th day. ; 21. The last sentence suggests that more may be learned about the Maya in the future. It is a good ending because it summarizes the article and hints at what may come next.

Day 3/Page 55: 1. $\frac{3}{10}$; 2. $\frac{4}{9}$; 3. $\frac{3}{16}$; 4. $\frac{10}{21}$; 5. $\frac{8}{35}$; 6. $\frac{1}{18}$; 7. $\frac{5}{36}$; 8. $\frac{1}{7}$; 9. $\frac{1}{4}$; 10. $\frac{2}{9}$; 11.–18. Answers will vary.; 19. chews; 20. cheap; 21. bear; 22. pale; 23. manor; 24. tiers; 25. pole; 26. lesson; 27. 16; 28. Boston Massacre, Boston Tea Party; 29. the Stamp Act, 9 years; 30. King George III; 31. Lexington and Concord

Day 4/Page 57: 1. C.; 2. F.; 3. A.; 4. E.; 5. B.; 6. D.; 7. $\frac{2}{9}$; 8. $\frac{15}{2}$; 9. $\frac{82}{7}$, 7, 5, 11 $\frac{5}{7}$; 10. improper, $5\frac{3}{5}$, $8\frac{3}{7}$; 11.–14. underline; 15.–17. no underline 18. underline; 19.–20. no underline; 21.–22. underline; 23.–25. no underline; 26. knew, new; 27. hour, our; 28. read; 29. buy, to; 30. their; 31. two 32. see, sea; 33. tail

Day 5/Page 59: 1. $1\frac{7}{8}$; 2. $1\frac{1}{2}$; 3. $\frac{2}{3}$; 4. 2; 5. $1\frac{1}{5}$; 6. $\frac{1}{3}$; 7. $1\frac{2}{7}$; 8. $\frac{2}{5}$; 9. $\frac{15}{16}$; 10. $5\frac{1}{4}$; 11. $2\frac{1}{3}$; 12. $1\frac{1}{9}$; 13. and; 14. but; 15. and; 16. or; 17. and; 18. but; 19. but; 20. and; 21. C.; 22. 4, 1, 3, 2; 23. She led American soldiers on a raid.; 24. Answers may include: helped the freed slaves, cared for the elderly, worked for women's rights.; 25. The author feels that Tubman is an American hero. The author uses words such as *strong* and *brave* to describe her.

Day 6/Page 61: 1. 30.41; 2. 24.683; 3. 9.096; 4. 19.14; 5. 451.606; 6. 342.325; 7. 51.841; 8. $107.02; 9.–15. Answers will vary.; 16. 1,900,000; 17. 0.000652; 18. 54,000,000; 19. 20,100; 20. 80,000,000; 21. 7,140; 22. 0.0000002; 23. 8.57; 24. 75,000,000,000; 25. 15,200; 26. 5,000,000; 27. 2.3548; 28. 89,510,000; 29. 700,000; 30. 12,598,000,000; Students' writing will vary.

Day 7/Page 63:

Date	Deposited	Withdrew	Total $
May 15	$500.25	$0	$500.25
May 31	$496.80	$0	$997.05
June 4	$0	$145.00	$852.05
June 15	$435.20	$0	$1,287.25
June 30	$600.00	$0	$1,887.25
July 1	$0	$463.00	$1,424.25
July 15	$110.00	$0	$1,534.25
July 24	$0	$600.00	$934.25

1. <u>iceburg</u>, iceberg; 2. <u>sieze</u>, seize; 3. <u>commitee</u>, committee; 4. <u>demacratic</u>; democratic; 5. <u>quotasion</u>, quotation; 6. <u>slugish</u>, sluggish; 7. <u>opress</u>, oppress; 8. <u>plack</u>, plaque; 9. –17. Answers will vary but may include: 9. mouth; 10. soup; 11. painting; 12. addresses; 13. gardener; 14. afternoon; 15. reasonable; 16. ad(vertisement); 17. school; Students' writing will vary.

Day 8/Page 65: 1. 7.055; 2. 0.7412; 3. 259.86; 4. 0.0117; 5. 0.518; 6. 0.207; 7. 0.0007; 8. 0.275; 9. S; 10. P; 11. H; 12. M; 13. S; 14. H; 15. P; 16. M; 17. Answers will vary. Possible answer: the wild geese crying "Spring! It is spring!"; 18. a loud ringing sound; 19. Answers will vary. Possible answer: The poet feels joyful. She is reflecting the joy she observes in nature. She writes about children dancing and singing, animals singing, and the cold weather leaving. She uses exclamations to show her excitement.

Day 9/Page 67: 1. 0.72; 2. 0.56; 3. 13.8; 4. 40.4; 5. 84.5; 6. 53.368; 7. 365.1232; 8. 512.05; 9. 498.852; 10. 2,514.255; 11. hand; 12. states; 13. foot; 14. go; 15. vine; 16. dog; 17. street (road); 18. den; 19. sculpture; 20. 60 m^3; 21. 160 in.^{3}; 22. 41.354 m^3; 23. 240 mm^3; 24. 38.4; in.^{3}; 25. $\frac{3}{32}$ in.^{3}

Day 10/Page 69: 1. 1.8; 2. 2.6; 3. 3.7; 4. 4.6; 5. 89; 6. 23.6; 7. 45.9; 8. 78.5; 9. 69.1; 10. 55.5; 11. their; 12. they; 13. they; 14. their; 15. she; 16. our; 17. they; 18. he or she; 19. Lowest value: 44, Highest value: 52, Spread: 8, Center value: 48; 20. Lowest value: 10, Highest value: 100, Spread: 90, Center value: 55; earthquake, energy, fault, fracture, focus, above, epicenter, beneath, Seismic waves, Seismologists

Day 11/Page 71: 1. 131.66; 2. 215.50; 3. 106,603; 4. 15,792; 5. 264,208; 6. 4,202,534; 7. 1,328.25; 8. 9,875.5; 9. $8\frac{1}{4}$; 10. $10\frac{1}{2}$; 11. $9\frac{3}{20}$; 12. $5\frac{1}{4}$; 13.–16. Answers will vary.; 17. Answers will vary. Possible answer: It seems like it will be a humorous story. Dr. Dolittle is an odd character who behaves strangely and has animals with funny names.; 18. The story is told from the third-person point of view. Answers will vary. Possible answer: If Dr. Dolittle told the story, the reader would know more about why he does what he does and what he is thinking.; 19. Answers will vary.

Day 12/Page 73: 1.–8. Order of answers may vary: 1. 56 × 39 = 2,184; 2,184 ÷ 39 = 56; 2,184 ÷ 56 = 39; 2. 37 × 95 = 3,515; 3,515 ÷ 37 = 95; 3,515 ÷ 95 = 37; 3. 76 × 49 = 3,724; 3,724 ÷ 76 = 49; 3,724 ÷ 49 = 76; 4. 27 × 151 = 4,077; 4,077 ÷ 27 = 151; 4,077 ÷ 151 = 27; 5. 3,762 ÷ 99 = 38; 99 × 38 = 3,762; 38 × 99 = 3,762; 6. 26,320 ÷ 560 = 47; 47 × 560 = 26,320; 560 × 47 = 26,320; 7. 48,306 ÷ 582 = 83; 83 × 582 =

147

48,306; 582 × 83 = 48,306; 8. 92 × 194 = 17,848; 17,848 ÷ 92 = 194; 17,848 ÷ 194 = 92; 9.–14. Answers will vary but may include: 9. She had a pleasant voice.; 10. The cat has smooth fur.; 11. The water is shiny and blue.; 12. Kristen absorbed the information.; 13. He stood straight.; 14. Answers will vary.; 15. 9; 16. 5; 17. 26; 18. 89; 19. 877; 20. 657; 21. 200; 22. 1,395; 23. 5,529; 24. 40; 25. 47,127; 26.190,498; Students' writing will vary.

Day 13/Page 75: 1.–8. Answers will vary but may include: 1. 5, 10, 15, 20, 25; 2. 18, 27, 36, 45, 54; 3. 20, 30, 40, 50, 60; 4. 24, 36, 48, 60, 72; 5. 12, 24, 36; 6. 10, 20, 30; 7. 28, 56, 84; 8. 24, 48, 72; 9. 18; 10. 12; 11. 30; 12. 40; 13.–20. Students should circle each word in orange: 13. **Carmen** ~~walks~~ carefully along the rocky shore.; 14. **Pools** of water ~~collect~~ in rocky crevices near the shore.; 15. Tide **pools** ~~are~~ home to sea plants and animals.; 16. **Seaweed** is the most common tide pool plant.; 17. **They** ~~provide~~ food and shelter for a variety of animals.; 18. **Carmen** ~~sees~~ spiny sea urchins attached to a rock.; 19. Their **mouths** ~~are~~ on their undersides.; 20. Their sharp **teeth** ~~cut~~ seaweed into little pieces.; 21.–25. Answers will vary.; 26. 6; 27. 17; 28. 1; 29. 20; 30. 35; 31. 34; 32. 4; 33. 38; 34. 74

Day 14/Page 77: 1. 2^4 = 16; 2. 8^3 = 512; 3. 4^6 = 4,096; 4. 3^4 = 81; 5. 9^3 = 729; 6. 10^7 = 10,000,000; 7. 5^5 = 3,125; 8. 7^3 = 343; 9. 6^4 = 1,296; 10.–17. Students should circle the words in orange: 10. CP, **planted, raised**; 11. CS, **Chinese, Japanese**; 12. N; 13. CS, **Fish, shellfish**; 14. CS, **Overfishing, pollution**; 15. CS, **Sea farming, ranching**; 16. CP, **raise, sell**; 17. CP, **grow, taste**; 18. C.; 19. land and other resources; 20. They were forced to move if settlers wanted their land.; 21. lands farther west (Oklahoma); 22. the long journey west that the Cherokees were forced to make; 23. Students' paragraphs will vary.

Day 15/Page 79: 1. herself; 2. ourselves; 3. yourself 4. himself; 5. yourselves; 6. myself; 7. ✔; 8. ✔; 9.

Shonda's book club, which meets on the first Tuesday of each month, is reading *Oliver Twist*.; 10. The old piano, which was badly in need of tuning, sat in the corner.; 11. ✔; 12. My grandmother attended Hawthorne Elementary, which was built in 1928.; 13. S, trees, soldiers; 14. S, cars, ants; 15. M, sound, dogs; 16. S, clowns, sardines; 17. M, feet, drums; 18. lines indicate darkest areas; 19. because one plate is pushed against another

Day 16/Page 81: 1. 128; 2. 14; 3. 19; 4. 26; 5. 30; 6. 26; 7. 126; 8. 26; 9. 20; 10. 64; 11. 432; 12. 12; 13. 104; 14. 840; 15. N: 95, 40; 16. M: 73, N: 68; 17. M: 70, N: 64, Rule: M − 9 = N; 18. M: 30, N: 13, Rule: M − 11 = N; 19. N: 60, 36, Rule: M × 6 = N; 20. N: 6, 4, Rule: M ÷ 3 = N; 21. M: 9, 6, Rule: M × 9 = N; 22. M: 12, 11, Rule: M × 12 = N; 23. Life, Liberty, and the pursuit of Happiness; 24. to secure the basic rights of people; 25. to alter it or abolish it and institute new Government

Day 17/Page 83: 1. 1, 2, 4, 8, 16; 1, 2, 4, 5, 8, 10, 20, 40, Students should circle both 8s.; 2. 1, 3, 9; 1, 2, 3, 4, 6, 12, Students should circle both 3s.; 3. 1, 2, 3, 4, 6, 8, 12, 24; 1, 2, 3, 6, 7, 14, 21, 42, Students should circle both 6s.; 4. 1, 2, 4, 8, 16, 32; 1, 2, 4, 11, 22, 44, Students should circle both 4s.; 5.–12. Students should circle words in orange: 5. **is** walking; 6. **has** shopped; 7. **might have** called, **had** known; 8. **is** closed; 9. **does** enjoy; 10. **is** playing; 11. **does** finish; 12. **are** watching; 13. B.; 14. World War II; 15. block proposals brought to the council by voting against them; 16. 5 years; 17. Answers may include: provides peacekeepers; helps victims of natural disasters; promotes workers' rights; provides food, medicine, and safe drinking water for those in need.

Day 18/Page 85: 1. $\frac{1}{2}$; 2. $\frac{4}{1}$; 3. $\frac{2}{3}$; 4. $\frac{11}{4}$; 5. $\frac{8}{3}$; 6. $\frac{4}{5}$; 7. The frogs sleep during the day, and they hunt for food at night.; 8. A parrot's bright colors are easy to see in a tree, but a tree boa's green color makes it difficult to spot.; 9. A fruit bat has a long nose, and it has large eyes to

help it see in the dark.; 10. I know math well.; 11. Who told the secret?; 12. He is just like his father.; 13. She will sleep very well tonight.; 14. The two friends are very similar.; 15. T; 16. T; 17. F; 18. F; 19. F; 20. T; 21. T; 22. F; 23. T

Day 19/Page 87: 1. 12 × 55 = (12 × 50) + (12 × 5) = 660; 2. 61 × 15 = (61 × 10) + (61 × 5) = 915; 3. 45 × 22 = (45 × 20) + (45 × 2) = 990; 4. 16 × 47 = (16 × 40) + (16 × 7) = 752; 5. 37 × 102 = (37 × 100) + (37 × 2) = 3,774; 6. 64 × 13 = (64 × 10) + (64 × 3) = 832; 7. 48 × 44 = (48 × 40) + (48 × 4) = 2,112; 8. 33 × 32 = (33 × 30) + (33 × 2) = 1,056; 9. C; 10. C; 11. A; 12. A; 13. B; 14. A.; Students' writing will vary.

Day 20/Page 89: 1. y × 12 = 108 when y = 9; 2. 36 ÷ b = 18 when b = 2; 3. w + 14 = 15 when w = 1; 4. (z × 6) ÷ 12 = 2 when z = 4; 5. c^2 × 2 = 50 when c = 5; 6. (15 − d) ÷ 4 = 2 when d = 7; 7. 23 + (x ÷ 6) = 25 when x = 12; Answers may vary. Possible answers: therm, heat; biannual; ology, study of; eruption, break; mono, one; ped; audience, to hear; ject; 8. C.; 9. to help predict future weather; 10. Answers may include: temperature, wind speed, atmospheric pressure, precipitation.; 11. They can predict how climate and weather might change in the future.; 12. when it might strike and how to stay safe; 13. Answers will vary.

Bonus Page 93: 1. opinion; 2. fact; 3. opinion; 4. fact; 5. opinion; 6. fact; 7. fact; 8. opinion

Bonus Page 94: 1. legislative; 2. legislative; 3. executive; 4. judicial; 5. executive; Pie chart will vary but may include: The executive branch carries out federal laws, recommends new laws, directs national defense and foreign policy, appoints justices, and performs ceremonial duties.; The legislative branch makes laws, passes laws, impeaches officials, and approves treaties.; The judicial branch interprets the Constitution, reviews laws, and decides cases involving states' rights.

Bonus Page 95: 1. Hawaii; 2. more

than 200 inches; 3. less than 8 inches; 4. more than 200 inches; 5. Kamuela; 6. Flagstaff; 7. Tucson, Phoenix; 8. Honokaa, Kailua-Kona

Section III

Day 1/Page 99: 1. 162 square in.; 2. 330 square in.; 3. 156 square cm; 4. 45 square mm; 5. 26 square cm; 6. 36 square mi.; 7. I; 8. me; 9. I; 10. me; 11. Her; 12. his; 13. My; 14. mine; 15. −5, −4, −3, −2, −1; 16. A.; 17. American Northwest

Day 2/Page 101: 1. OP; 2. SP; 3. OP; 4. SP; 5. SP; 6. SP; 7. SP; 8. OP; 9. OP; 10. SP; 11. 12; 12. 7; 13. 15; 14. 23; 15. 105; 16. 48; 17. 17; 18. 3; 19. 62; 20. 14; 21. 29; 22. 82; 23.−24. Answers will vary.; 25. dramatize, dra-me-tīz; 26. 3; 27. to behave dramatically; 28.−29. Answers will vary.; Students' writing will vary.

Day 3/Page 103: 1. 55; 2. 3.9; 3. 28¢; 4. $\frac{3}{4}$ inch; 5. 48; 6. 17¢; 7. 26¢; 8. 1,900; 9. $4.50; 10. $1.35; 11.−24. Sample words will vary. Possible answers are shown: 11. A, chronology, chronic; 12. B, astronaut, astronomy; 13. A, sympathy, empathy; 14. C, biology, biography; 15. C.; 16. to buy stamps and mail letters and packages; 17. on foot, by car, by truck, or by airplane; 18. a country's national post office; 19. the size and weight of an item, the distance to its destination, and its target delivery date

Day 4/Page 105: 1. $16y$; 2. $60y − 36$; 3. $40g + 16$; 4. $x^2 + 8x$; 5. $75 − 100n$; 6. $32z$; 7. $32x + 52$; 8. $15y + 65$; 9. $8w^2 − 16$; 10. $45c − 30$; 11. $18k − 42$; 12. $12 ÷ 3a$; 13.−16. Answers will vary.; 17. yes; 18. yes; 19. no; 20. no; 21. yes; 22. yes; 23. yes; 24. yes; 25. no; 26. yes; 27. yes; 28. no; 29. yes; 30. no; 31. no

Day 5/Page 107:
1. $z > 2$,

2. $y < 4$,

3. $d ≥ −1$,

4. $a < −2$,

5. $c ≤ −8$,

6. $w > 3$,

7. d; 8. h; 9. a; 10. f; 11. g; 12. c; 13. e; 14. b; 15. horse; 16. music; 17. home; 18. story; 19. young tree; 20. clothing; 21. 63; 22. 28; 23. 56; 24. 52.$\overline{3}$

Day 6/Page 109: 1. 54 bars of soap; 2. 40 points; 3. 240 miles; 4. $9.60, $14.40; 5. $7.50, $17.50; 6. $12, $68; 7. $132, $88; 8. $49.50, $40.50; 9. $54, $66; 10. $312.50, $937.50; 11. C; 12. for religious freedom or for more land for their families; 13. horses, oxen, and sheep; 14. in one-room schoolhouses or at home; 15. doctor's office, blacksmith's shop, general store

Day 7/Page 111: 1. 1; 2. 1.5 or $1\frac{1}{2}$; 3. 24; 4. 4; 5. 2; 6. 21; 7. 36; 8. 3; 9. 9; 10. 0.5 or $\frac{1}{2}$; 11. 30; 12. 132; 13.−18. Answers will vary. Possible answers: 13. "I really enjoyed the concert," said Marissa.; 14. That construction across the street is bothering me a great deal.; 15. I appreciate you telling me the recent news.; 16. We only have a few minutes before the bell, so you have to do it as soon as possible.; 17. A large traffic jam caused traffic to slow down for quite some time.; 18. Their family is wealthy, so the cost of the tickets will not be a problem for them.; 19.−21. Answers will vary but may include: 19. The Table of Contents is arranged by chapters. The Index is arranged alphabetically by subject.; 20. in the Index; 21. in the Table of Contents, Chapter Six, page 260; 22. 5; 23. 172

Day 8/Page 113: 1. 250; 2. 3,000; 3. 900; 4. 1,000; 5. 12,000; 6. 800; 7. 5; 8; 10,000; 9. 400,000; Answers will vary.; 10. Timbuktu is a small trading town in central Mali.; 11. it was a trading post for products from North and West Africa; 12. It is not as important or populated as it once was.; 13. 54; 14. 90; 15. 158; 16.112; 17. 960; 18. 216

Day 9/Page 115: 1. 2; 2. 48; 3. 0.5 or $\frac{1}{2}$; 4. 0.25 or $\frac{1}{4}$; 5. 2,000; 6. 2; 7. 1; 8. 6; 9. 1; 10. 1; 11. 1; 12. 0.625 or $\frac{1}{16}$; Answers will vary but may include:
1624 Bay Lane
Short Creek, PA 12525
May 10, 2015

Dear Aunt Ann and Uncle James,

    School will soon be out for the summer. I am looking forward to it. The year was good, and I learned a lot.

    Mom and Dad are going to France in July. I don't want to go with them. I'm writing this letter to ask if I can stay with you July 10 through July 22. I would love to help you take care of the horses and do anything else that you would want me to do. I would also help around the house. Please let me know if I can come.

                Your loving niece,
                Julie Ann

13. 3, 1, 2, 4; 14. Pulitzer Prize; 15. people who lived in the part of Chicago where she lived; 16. Answers will vary.

Day 10/Page 117: 1. 1; 2. 1; 3. 4,000; 4. 5,000; 5. 3; 6. 9,000; 7. 8,000; 8. 4; 9. 9,500; 10. 2,000,000; 11. 9; 12. 7,000,000; Answers will vary.; 13.−14. Answers will vary.; 15. heating and pressure; 16. melting and crystallization; 17. sedimentation and compaction; 18. heating and pressure; 19. melting and crystallization; 20. sedimentation and compaction

Day 11/Page 119: 1. 20%; 2. 50%; 3. 8%; 4. 47%; 5. 9%; 6. $\frac{19}{100}$; 7. $\frac{24}{100}$; 8. $\frac{87}{100}$; 9. $\frac{36}{100}$; 10. $\frac{99}{100}$; 11. $\frac{1}{2}$; 12. $\frac{9}{10}$; 13. $\frac{1}{5}$; 14. $\frac{9}{20}$; 15. $\frac{7}{10}$; 16. This year, on my mom's birthday (June 14th), we will have a family picnic.; 17. Jones hit the ball—way into left field—and the crowd went wild.; 18. The new puppy, a cocker spaniel, got tangled up in her leash.; 19.−23. Answers will vary but may include: 19. pretended; 20. coworkers; 21. on time; 22. stamp collector; 23. rouse; 3, 1, 2, 4

Day 12/Page 121: 1. $\frac{5}{7}$; 2. $\frac{20}{13}$; 3. $\frac{12}{5}$; 4. $\frac{4}{9}$; 5. 23¢/45¢; 6. $\frac{10}{3}$; 7. $\frac{1}{4}$

; 8. $\frac{3}{25}$; 9. $\frac{2}{3}$; 10. $\frac{3}{2}$; 11. $\frac{3}{3}$; 12. $\frac{3}{8}$; 13. regions; 14. grip; 15. primates; 16. termites; 17. pokes; 18. plucks; 19. charge, ripping; 20. bounds; 21. A; 22. The author's purpose is to explain what geologists do and why it is important. This is evident because the author provides supporting facts and examples.; 23. movement of plates on Earth's crust, volcanoes, earthquakes, movement of glaciers; 24. to help plants grow better; 25. interpret data

Day 13/Page 123: I. country; 2. jazz; 3. 175; 4. 157.14285; 5. Answers will vary.; 6. gigantic; 7. ornately; 8. audience; 9. thirty-year-old; 10. enormous; II. completely; 12. magnificently; 13. brilliantly; 14. enthusiastically; 15. splendid; 16. sluggish and lazy (dashes); 17. flat-bladed ax (phrase); 18. highly-seasoned stew (commas); 19. kneecap (phrase); 20. xylophone (parentheses)

Day 14/Page 125: I. $2.50; 2. $4.00; 3. $5.00; 4. $6.00; 5.–10. Answers will vary but may include: 5. The team didn't want any trouble.; 6. Haven't you ever seen Yellowstone National Park?; 7. There aren't any eggs in the carton.; 8. He wasn't near any base when he was tagged out.; 9. There isn't any way to get there from here.; 10. The explanation didn't make any sense.; II. $1\frac{1}{5}$; 12. 2; 13. $\frac{2}{9}$; 14. $\frac{3}{4}$; 15. B.; 16. D.; 17. C.; 18. A.; 19. E.

Day 15/Page 127: I. Monday; 2. 10 family members; 3. 250; 4. Wednesday; 5. 55; 6. Answers will vary.; 7.–11. Answers will vary but may include: 7. Can't anyone solve the puzzle?; 8. Rick didn't have anything to read.; 9. Annie had never seen that.; 10. Don't spill any of the juice.; II. There isn't anything you can do about it.; 12. A; 13. 2, 4, 1, 3; 14. New Orleans; 15. admiral

Day 16/Page 129: 2. (4, 4); 5. (–9, –4); 8. trapezoid;

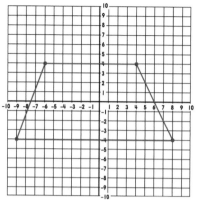

Today, the term "American Indian" is used to describe people indigenous to **America. However,** the **first** explorers who came to America referred to them as **"Indians."** **Unknown** to the explorers, most tribes had their own names. **For example,** the name used by the **Delaware Indians** of eastern **North America** meant "genuine men." **The** Indians' **languages,** ways of life, and homes **were** all very different. The **Aztec** and **Maya** Indians of **Central America** built large **cities.** The **Apache** and Paiute used brushes and **matting** to make simple **huts. The Plains Indians built cone-shaped** tepees covered with buffalo **skins.** Cliff **Dwellers** and other Pueblo groups **used** sun-dried bricks to make many **storied houses.**; 9.–12. Answers will vary but may include: 9. so, snow, white ground; 10. so, electricity went out, went out to dinner; II. so, unlatched gate, cattle were in the road; 12. so, Scott had the flu, he had to miss school; 13. D; 14. B; 15. C; 16. A

Day 17/Page 131: 1. 9; 2. 0; 3. –8; 4. 4; 5. –2; 6. <; 7. >; 8. >; 9. <; 10. >; II. >; 12.–15. Answers will vary but may include: 12. Jim, Sean, and Maria liked to visit Grandma and Grandpa.; 13. Grandpa had horses, cows, and goats on his farm.; 14. Grandma raised chickens, ducks, and geese.; 15. Daisies, tulips, and roses grew in her garden.; 16. –25. Answers will vary.

Day 18/Page 133: I. (multiples of 4) 4, 8, 12, 16; (multiples of 4 and 5) 0, 20; (multiples of 5) 5, 10, 15, 25; 2.

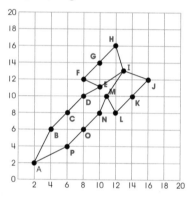

3. his; 4. her; 5. my; 6. her; 7. their; 8. your; 9. Answers will vary.; 10. Answers will vary. Possible answer: The poet is remembering a time in his life when he made a choice and is grateful that he chose the path he did.; II. Answers will vary. Possible answer: The poet looks back on his life and is thankful for the path he chose.

Day 19/Page 135: 1.–4.

5. Who; 6. Whom; 7. Who; 8. Who; 9. Who; 10. Who; II. Whom; 12. who; 13. whom; 14. whom; 15. <u>trophy</u>, proudly stood; 16. <u>clouds</u>, spit icicles; 17. <u>leaves</u>, sing, danced; 18. <u>Horns</u>, honked angrily; 19. <u>sun</u>, played hide-and-seek; Students' writing will vary.

Day 20/Page 137:

I.

2. 25; 3. 15; 4. 35; 5. lie; 6. can; 7. may; 8. can; 9. may; 10. lay; II. B; 12. B; 13. C; 14. A; 15. A; 16. C; 17. D; 18. C; 19. G; 20. F; 21. A; 22. B; 23. E

Bonus Page 141: I. G; 2. D; 3. C; 4. E; 5. F; 6. B; 7. A; 8. 50, District; 9. democracy, president; 10. legislature, governor

Bonus Page 142: I. no; 2. no; 3. yes; 4. yes; 5. no; 6. no; 7. no; 8. yes

Bonus Page 143: I. false; 2. true; 3. false; 4. true; 5. false; 6. true; 7. false; 8. true; 9. true; 10. false

struct
(make, build)

port
(carry)

meter
(measure)

aster, astr
(star)

dict
(say, speak)

spect
(watch,
look at)

tract
(draw, pull)

fact
(do, make)

form
(shape)

thermometer
barometer

portable
import
report

construct
structure
destruction

spectacle
inspect
respect

predict
dictionary
dictate

astronomy
asteroid
asterisk

deformed
inform
formation

factory
manufacture

retract
tractor
subtract

phon
(sound)

auto
(self)

min
(less, smaller)

Red is to colors as nine is to _____.

Egg is to dozen as mitten is to _____.

Glass is to shatter as bubble is to _____.

Too is to two as made is to _____.

Excited is to bored as right is to _____.

Bush is to shrub as chair is to _____.

phonics
telephone
microphone

autobiography
automobile
automatic

minute
minuscule
minority

Red is to *colors* as
nine is to <u>numbers</u>.

Egg is to *dozen* as
mitten is to <u>pair</u>.

Glass is to *shatter* as
bubble is to <u>pop</u>.

Too is to *two* as
made is to <u>maid</u>.

Excited is to *bored*
as *right* is to <u>left</u>.

Bush is to *shrub* as
chair is to <u>seat</u>.

Lion is to *pride* as
dog is to
_____.

© Carson-Dellosa

Pool is to *water* as
balloon is to
_____.

© Carson-Dellosa

Mountain is to
avalanche as ocean
is to
_____.

© Carson-Dellosa

Tree is to *leaf* as
hand is to
_____.

© Carson-Dellosa

Hat is to *head* as
roof is to
_____.

© Carson-Dellosa

Lightbulb is to *socket*
as key is to
_____.

© Carson-Dellosa

Choose is to *chews* as
grown is to
_____.

© Carson-Dellosa

Water is to *fire* as
eraser is to
_____.

© Carson-Dellosa

Frame is to *painting* as
pedestal is to
_____.

© Carson-Dellosa

Lion is to *pride* as
dog is to __pack__ .

Pool is to *water* as
balloon is to __air__ .

Mountain is to *avalanche*
as ocean is to __hurricane__ .

Tree is to *leaf* as
hand is to __finger__ .

Hat is to *head* as
roof is to __house__ .

Lightbulb is to *socket*
as key is to __lock__ .

Choose is to *chews* as
grown is to __groan__ .

Water is to *fire* as
eraser is to __writing__ .

Frame is to *painting* as
pedestal is to __statue__ .

Letter is to *word* as *word* is to _____.

© Carson-Dellosa

simile

© Carson-Dellosa

metaphor

© Carson-Dellosa

personification

© Carson-Dellosa

idiom

© Carson-Dellosa

proverb

© Carson-Dellosa

There are 3 cups of flour for each cup of sugar. Give the ratio.

© Carson-Dellosa

A car drives 60 miles in 1 hour. Give the ratio.

© Carson-Dellosa

There are 3 parrots and 5 parakeets in a cage. Give the ratio.

© Carson-Dellosa

Hector was a torpedo shooting through the water as he swam.

© Carson-Dellosa

The pads on the kitten's paw looked like little pink erasers.

© Carson-Dellosa

Letter is to word as word is to sentence.

© Carson-Dellosa

A picture is worth a thousand words.

© Carson-Dellosa

Mikki knew the money she had saved so far was just a drop in the bucket if she hoped to buy a new computer.

© Carson-Dellosa

The palm trees quietly danced in the ocean breeze.

© Carson-Dellosa

3 to 5

3:5

or $\frac{3}{5}$

© Carson-Dellosa

60 to 1

60:1

or $\frac{60}{1}$

© Carson-Dellosa

3 to 1

3:1

or $\frac{3}{1}$

© Carson-Dellosa

There are 2 trucks and 7 cars in a parking lot. Give the ratio.

$\frac{3}{10} = \underline{\quad} \%$

$\frac{18}{25} = \underline{\quad} \%$

$\frac{63}{100} = \underline{\quad} \%$

$\frac{15}{30} = \underline{\quad} \%$

Find the greatest common factor of 63 and 84.

Find the greatest common factor of 75 and 30.

Find the greatest common factor of 45 and 48.

Find the least common multiple of 3 and 9.

$\frac{18}{25} = \underline{72}\,\%$

$\frac{3}{10} = \underline{30}\,\%$

2 to 7

2:7

or $\frac{2}{7}$

21

$\frac{15}{30} = \underline{50}\,\%$

$\frac{63}{100} = \underline{63}\,\%$

9

3

15

Find the least
common multiple
of 9 and 12.

© Carson-Dellosa

Find the least
common multiple
of 6 and 8.

© Carson-Dellosa

-4 $\bigcirc$ 3

© Carson-Dellosa

7 $\bigcirc$ -8

© Carson-Dellosa

5 $\bigcirc$ -5

© Carson-Dellosa

-6 $\bigcirc$ -1

© Carson-Dellosa

-9 $\bigcirc$ -12

© Carson-Dellosa

15 $\bigcirc$ -12

© Carson-Dellosa

$[(25 - 14) \times 8] + 7 =$

© Carson-Dellosa

-4 < 3

© Carson-Dellosa

24

© Carson-Dellosa

36

© Carson-Dellosa

-6 < -1

© Carson-Dellosa

5 > -5

© Carson-Dellosa

7 > -8

© Carson-Dellosa

$[(25 - 14) \times 8] + 7 = 95$

© Carson-Dellosa

15 > -12

© Carson-Dellosa

-9 > -12

© Carson-Dellosa

$12 \times [9 - (15 \div 5)] =$

$(3 \times 4^2) \div 8 =$

$(54 \div 2) + (42 \div 7) =$

$(2^3 \times 5) - 15 =$

9 cm

6 cm

Find the area.

$1\frac{1}{2}$ in.

$2\frac{1}{3}$ in.

$\frac{3}{4}$ in.

Find the volume.

2 mm

4 mm

4 mm

9 mm

Find the area.

12 ft.

16 ft.

Find the area.

$\frac{2}{3}$ m

$\frac{7}{8}$ m

$\frac{9}{10}$ m

Find the volume.

$12 \times [9 - (15 \div 5)] = 72$

$(3 \times 4^2) \div 8 = 6$

$(54 \div 2) + (42 \div 7) = 33$

$(2^3 \times 5) - 15 = 25$

Area =
27 square
centimeters

Volume =
$2\frac{5}{8}$ cubic
inches

Area =
36 square
millimeters

Area =
192 square
feet

Volume =
$\frac{21}{40}$ cubic
meters

Summer Bridge Activities®

Congratulations!

This certifies that

_____
Name

has completed **Summer Bridge Activities**.

_____
Parent's Signature